Joshua

One Man's Journey to Salvation

Philip Antony

Illustrations by Mackenzie Rose Ridgeway

For my beloved Sara Jean –
My editor, best friend, and soul mate

Acknowledgments

I wish to thank the two people who contributed to bringing this story to fruition. Special thanks to Claire Cieslewicz for her interest in the project, for her reading and editing the first draft. Many thanks also to my dear friend, Moshe Banai, for helping with the geography of Israel, and ensuring that I remained true to the Hebrew references in the Bible. Both Moshe and Claire are former teachers, whose numerous edits spared me any embarrassment owing to my grammar and spelling deficiencies.

It is with enormous gratitude and sadness that I acknowledge the contribution of Sara Jean who was my first and most critical editor; who helped with the numerous re-writes; and who gave me the encouragement to continue to write not only this story, but also many others. Sadly, she is no longer with us, and will be sadly missed as my best editor, friend and wife.

Contents

PROLOGUE

He started life with a severe handicap, endured crippling pain, a harsh life, shunned by many, but in the end discovered that his life gave true meaning to his Hebrew name, Joshua: 'God is Salvation.' It is said that adversity has two alternative outcomes: despair or greatness. It is a binary choice that one makes when confronted by hardship and misfortune: either despair, wither and die, or overcome, fight and achieve great things. History has recorded those that succeeded, and forgotten those who have succumbed to their troubles. This is the story of Joshua who was born into adversity, struggled but rose beyond despair. He achieved more than greatness.

He achieved salvation.

CHAPTER 1

Kfar Nahum was a small fishing hamlet on the north shore of the Sea of Galilee, a short distance from the town of Gennesaret. The sea provided an abundance of fish that the villagers could sell or barter. The mud and brick houses, although modest in size, were comfortable. The gentle breeze off the sea made the desert heat of the day bearable; the nights made for good sleeping. The houses themselves were randomly scattered to provide space for vegetable gardens where the villagers grew corn, barley, dates, figs and vegetables. Olive and lemon trees and grape vines completed each villager's back garden. In the hills just beyond the village, older boys tended the flock of sheep that were owned in common by the members. Little children played and sang along the shore whilst their fathers tended fishing nets, and sewed sails. Women tended the gardens, cooked for the community, and served as the heart and soul of every family.

The air was redolent with the scent of grapes crushed for wine. Olive presses ensured that every person in the village had oil for cooking, grooming and treatments for various skin conditions. The people of the village celebrated their holidays, led by Rabbi Judah ben Shmuel Halevi, with song and prayer. The days were filled with joy and hope for the future. The residents of the hamlet had lived there for generations in peace and harmony. All of the day's activities were communal affairs, so were the other joys and sorrows of life in this idyllic place. Yes, life was good.

Until, it wasn't…

No one could explain it. Was it a curse? Punishment by God? What once was a small slice of paradise had now become a hellish furnace. The sun beat down on Kfar Nahum and all the towns and villages on the border of the Sea of Galilee with relentless fury for months on end. No one could explain what caused the ferocious heat. Some said it was punishment for the villagers who had lost their way and fallen into faithless existence, neglecting to give thanks to the Lord for the good fortune of the people of Kfar Nahum. Others attributed this misfortune to a black spirit that had covered the land like a dark blanket. Regardless of the cause for such prolonged misery, many did not care about the reason – only survival mattered. Now the villagers moved as if in slow motion, and then only from one shady spot to another. An ominous silence had settled over the houses. Even speaking took too much energy. Several of the elders of the village had already succumbed to the scorching sun. The children were nowhere to be seen. The shepherd boys on the hill had abandoned the sheep.

No, there would be no fishing today, not tomorrow and not for the foreseeable future, so intense was the heat. The water of the sea was completely still; it resembled a gigantic mirror reflecting the heat of the sun. In this heat, the fish went into the deepest depths of the sea. Only a fool would attempt to fish in such conditions, particularly when both sails and nets were useless – no wind, no fish, no food – just certain death.

The conditions on shore were no better. In the distance, one could see the waves of heat rising on the sandy hills. Well, water was now mixed with mud, a sure sign that the supply was at the point of exhaustion. The once plentiful patches of corn, vegetables and fruits had shriveled and died as if thrown into an oven. The abundant fig trees, grape vines and olive trees were scorched and withered. The villagers could only wait, wait for the weather to break, or die.

It was in the blistering heat of the noonday sun that a male child was born to Ethan and Deborah. Today should have been a joyous occasion to celebrate another Jewish member of Kfar Nahum with rituals and festivities. However, it turned out that both the blazing heat and nature had conspired to make this day the beginning of a life of pain and exclusion for this child that would last for a lifetime.

His name was Joshua. His Hebrew name means 'God is Salvation.' Little could anyone know at the time of his birth how auspicious that name would become in Judeo-Christian history.

The little infant was wrapped in swaddling, and fed from his mother's breast. One morning as the wraps were removed, the excited infant reached for his mother. At that moment, his mother saw that only one of his legs moved. The other lay limp. She gently lifted the limp leg, but it fell back as if it was lifeless. It was now painfully clear that the child's left leg was completely useless.

Nonetheless, his mother, Deborah, and his father, Ethan, celebrated the birth. He was circumcised according to the law, and as was the custom, his parents prepared a modest feast for the other villagers with music, dancing and singing. Most of the villagers excused themselves despite their hunger and thirst. As Deborah was assisted by the other women of the village during the birth, the whispers revealed what everyone already knew: Joshua was without the use of one of his limbs. His future was uncertain. Suspicion and fear mixed with ignorance rendered their home either cursed or damned. It was better to avoid such a house lest a similar fate would befall their children. Every member was considered an integral unit in order for the village to prosper and grow. Without both legs, he could not work on the boats; he could not farm, and certainly could not tend the sheep and goats with the other young boys. What role could such a useless person play in the village?

Despite his inauspicious entry to the world, and a birth that was marred by suspicion and fear, his parents loved him, and accepted the little boy's condition as a sign from God. It was a sign that rather than being a hopeless cripple, Joshua was a special child endowed by God with extraordinary gifts that would be revealed in due course.

Throughout his life, he struggled to walk as the paralysis was accompanied by intense spasms of pain as well. A few steps would leave him gasping in agony. One could easily see that his young face was etched in searing pain, leaving him with a face much older than his years. It was only through sheer grit and determination that he took his first halting steps despite falling over numerous times. He cried as the pain shot up through his spine. Lying on the floor from one of his many falls, he cried from having to struggle, but that only made him all the more resolute to overcome this adversity.

Joshua's early years were spent almost entirely confined to a bed of straw. When he heard the sound of children playing in the village square – something he would never be able to do – tears welled up in his eyes. He turned his face to the wall hoping that the laughter would fall silent. When Joshua was five, his father, a carpenter by trade, fashioned a crude crutch for his little son that allowed him to learn to walk. Against the wall where his bed stood was the mute chronicle of his life's history in the form of the various sizes of crutches he used.

Despite numerous painful and frustrating attempts to walk, he did manage to hobble about, which often ended with tottering in a heap. His world consisted of daily walks from his bed of straw to a turn in the garden and then back again. It was a small world for Joshua, but it was a world filled with wonder. His mother or father accompanied him for these short perambulations, and as they did, they described the wonders of the lemon tree, the fig tree and the beautiful flowers with their enchanting fragrances. Sadly, however, he could only imagine this world of beauty as most of these trees and flowers had been scorched by the heat.

"Look, Joshua, see this was once a fig tree. Its fruits are sweet; it nourishes the body, and here, my child, is what remains of the lemon tree. Although its fruits are sour, it too is a gift from God. Everything that you see is an extension of God. It is God's love that provides this nourishment."

His parents' voices were soft and tender, and gave Joshua encouragement and confidence to understand that his 'disorder' as some villagers called it, was a sign that he was not a hopeless cripple, but rather, a person with special gifts. Joshua loved these daily walks despite the unforgiving heat. He could only imagine the beauty, the fragrance and the abundance of these gifts. Unlike most of the other children in the village, who just wanted to fill their bellies and play, Joshua wanted to know more than just the taste of the fruits. His thirst for knowledge was insatiable.

"Father, how are these grown? Please describe every flower and tree. When is the fruit ripe? How does one tend to these gifts?" For his part, Joshua's father patiently explained to his son that it was a combination of love and care, good weather, and God's grace that produced such wealth.

Joshua was shunned by the other children in the village. He was an outcast, ostracized and abused. On the infrequent occasions that he ventured outside the confines of the garden, the other children would throw stones at him and beat him with sticks. He was called 'cursed' and 'evil.' Fearing he might be hurt, his mother and father kept him within the walls of their home except for his regular visits to the synagogue.

Joshua had two older brothers, Seth and Aaron, both of whom treated him cruelly as well. They were jealous of the attention that the little boy received and resentful that, for years, they had to shoulder the grueling work in the fields. One morning as the brothers were leaving for the fields, Aaron looked directly at Joshua and, with a voice dripping with disdain, said, "You are a useless and worthless human being, if you can call yourself human."

From Seth came an even more unkind cut, "I wish you were dead."

For his entire youth, they rejected him; he could not understand their cruelty and rejection. Joshua so wanted their love and attention. Despite the numerous challenges he faced, the rejection and exclusion only made Joshua more determined to press on.

He grew up to become so tall that he towered over all the others in the village. As such, he had a commanding presence. His dark curly hair tumbled over his shoulders like water flowing over rocks. Ignoring the custom of men of his time, he did not grow a beard. Although young, his face was dark and weathered from his long days in the sun. The most striking feature of his face was his dark, deep set of eyes that could be unnerving and betrayed the warmth and caring that really defined him. Owing to the life-long use of crutches, he had become very muscular and remarkably agile. Eventually, he managed to get about with the crutches with ease, to the surprise of many. His one and only friend, Moshe, had long ago distanced himself from the other boys. The two could spend every day together, and still find enough talk and play to fill the time. Moshe taught his lanky friend to play football, or at least a clumsy, almost comical version of it. It was a testament to their mutual trust and friendship. They could laugh when Joshua's 'stick' came out from under him in an awkward attempt to kick a goal and fell in a heap that sent his crutch flying.

CHAPTER 2

The years passed quietly for Joshua. They were mixed with both pain and rejection. Apart from Moshe and his parents, Joshua led a very quiet, almost solitary life. Despite his isolation, he could escape into his garden where the fragrance of a few surviving flowers and the song of birds filled him with inexpressible joy. For at least a few moments, Joshua would be in a magical world, feeling the wonders of nature and communion with God.

One day, Joshua awoke to the sounds of cheers, songs and praises to God and even gaiety, a sound he had never heard before in the village. He lifted himself from his bed and hobbled to the door. To his amazement, there were dark clouds spilling down the hills behind the village. Many of the villagers danced in the steady rain and splashed like children in the rivulets that had formed in the village center. Indeed, it was a joyous moment. The years of famine, misery and death were over; their prayers had been answered. Never having felt rain before, Joshua took several hesitant steps. The rain was falling in torrents. He felt the water on his face and opened his mouth to taste this mystery. He rubbed his face and ran his fingers through his matted hair, and felt the tingle of water rolling down his back. It was exhilarating! Soon thereafter, the lemon and olive trees came back to life; the flowers sprouted, lifting their faces to the deep blue sky, and the wells were once again filled with sweet groundwater. The sea cooled and produced an abundance of fish. Now there was enough food for all in the village. The young boys once again tended their sheep. The villagers celebrated under the stars, feasting and singing songs of praise for their deliverance from the misery that had engulfed them for so long. Surely this was a sign from the Lord God.

Joshua grew into a quiet and serious boy. He could only help tend the garden and help his mother in the kitchen with the cooking. It was noticeable that under his care, together with the rains, supplemented with numerous trips to the well, the garden produced a bounty of vegetables and fruits. Now, he discovered the tastes that had eluded him for so many years. Yes, the figs were sweet, as were the grapes, the pressed green olives had their distinctive taste, and lemons were indeed sour but delicious nonetheless. His favorite was the figs that he consumed in large quantities much to the concern of his mother. The birds watched him unafraid; he had a beautiful voice and would sing to the plants, flowers and trees. His parents provided him with handwritten scrolls of the day. In his visits with the rabbis, he quickly learned the Bible, the languages of the day, and managing money. He was a quick student who loved learning.

His garden was soon the envy of the village. With his mother's guidance, he could prepare a meal equal to any woman in the village. From his father, he learned the trade of a carpenter. With the return of the fish, Joshua's carpentry skills were sought after by many in the area, especially the fishermen requiring the repair of their boats. With his Bible studies together with the lively exchanges with the temple rabbis, he also proved to be an intellectually agile student, articulate and a masterful debater.

With the passing years, Joshua was no longer seen as the 'cripple' and a pariah. Now the other villagers, except for his brothers, realized that Joshua was not a cursed child after all, but rather a special and gifted one. He was soft-spoken, gentle and compassionate. He gave freely of his time to anyone who asked. Many asked for his guidance in understanding passages in the Bible; many more sought help for managing a garden. He became admired by everyone, especially among the young children. They hung on every word of his. It was not uncommon for him to invite the children into his garden to share its beauty, sweet scents, and the mystery that God played in it. The sweet songs and squeals of laughter of the children enchanted the villagers. He taught the children to pray and sing songs of praise to God for His love and grace. However, it was not all prayer. With the help of Moshe, they organized a small football pitch, and could only watch with amazement how Joshua deftly managed with one leg and one crutch to make a goal.

Early one morning, Joshua thought he heard his mother's voice as if in a dream, "Joshua, Joshua, please come to me."

No, it wasn't a dream. As he approached her bed, Joshua could see that there was something very wrong. She should have been up and about at this hour.

"Joshua, my son, I am unable to get up from my bed. Please help me."

She was pale; her breathing was shallow as she struggled to get up. The thing that struck Joshua was her eyes. They had lost their luster; they were glassy and almost fixed in the middle, unmoving. He leaned over and, almost in a whisper, asked her, "Mother, what ails you? What is it that I can do for you?"

He struggled to help her up. As he did so, she cried out in pain. Even with his strength, he could not lift her. She had become dead weight. He gently laid her back, whereupon she heaved a big sigh after what seemed to her as a herculean task to get up. Tears welled in Joshua's eyes. Seeing the worry and fear on his face, his mother slowly, painfully reached up and touched his face to reassure him.

"It's all right, my son, all will be well, but I think it is better that I remain here."

Then she closed her eyes and fell into a fitful sleep. When he stepped back, a crushing weight fell on him. He knew that she was not getting out of that bed - ever. He felt so helpless. All his life, he was able to control or adapt to any situation. He retreated to a corner of her room, sat down, brought up his knees to his chest, and began to sob uncontrollably. How could this be? Why? She was a virtuous and pure soul who gave of herself without measure. And now this? Over and over, he asked himself the same question: *why? Was there something I could have done to make her life easier? Did my life put too much of a strain on her?* So many questions but no answers.

The local physician came, but he was unable to determine the cause of her illness. It was clear to him that the situation was dire.

"It is not good; I think this is now in the hands of God."

Within a matter of weeks after the physician's visit, his mother's health continued to deteriorate. Joshua looked after her day and night, tending to her every need. He had taken to sleeping in her room lest he missed her call. During his many sleepless nights, he listened to her breathing, which was mixed with cries of agony. Joshua slowly and painfully accepted that it was hopeless. Through his tears, he prayed to God, not really knowing what he was praying for, a last-minute cure for his mother, a peaceful death? Try as he might, he could not summon the strength to face his beloved mother's death; she had played such a pivotal role in his young life. Late one morning, she called for him. "Joshua, please call your father and your brothers. I fear my time has come."

They surrounded her cot and alternatively prayed and spoke to her. In these last moments, she looked at them and gently smiled. She beckoned her husband to come closer. She took his hand and whispered in his ear, "My beloved husband, you gave me three sons, a home and the other simple pleasures of life. I could not have asked for more. I love you."

Then she took one last look at her sons, especially Joshua and closed her eyes. Her breath became slower and more labored until it stopped. Her pain and agony were over; she was free.

His father began to tremble, and then falling to his knees, cried out, "My Lord God, you have taken away the other half of me. Why did you not take me? She was pure and blameless in your sight, a jewel in your crown, and a priceless gift to me. Why, my Lord? What am I to do without my Deborah?"

His two sons, Seth and Aaron, gently helped him to his feet. Aaron, the younger of the two brothers, put his arm around his father.

"Come, father, take heart, our mother is now in peace. Her suffering has ended; she has been reunited with God our Father."

Ethan took one last, long look at his beloved Deborah. He leaned over and gently kissed her forehead as tears streamed onto her face.

"Goodbye, my beloved. Wait for me; soon, we shall be together forever."

The two brothers escorted him to the courtyard. His shoulders were stooped; and he walked as if his legs were too heavy. His head rolled around like a puppet on a string. Over and over, he kept muttering something unintelligible.

With the help of the two brothers, he managed to shuffle to a crude bench under a lemon tree. Seth looked at Aaron and said, "Brother, let us leave him to his grief. We can do nothing more for him."

Ethan remained hunched over, alternately sobbing, and through his tears, asked over and over, "Why, my God, why?" It was late in the afternoon that the two brothers returned, finding him still bent over, rocking back and forth. With great effort, they helped him to his bed.

Joshua was left alone with his mother. The lines of pain and agony were gone. It seemed to Joshua that in death, her youthful face had returned. She looked so peaceful. He wanted to keep that picture of her in his mind forever. He sat there for the longest time looking at her and holding her hand. He had no idea how much time had passed, and were it not for the pain of sitting for hours, he could have stayed longer. He slowly rose, stretched his muscles and rubbed his neck. He looked down at his mother for the longest time.

"I cannot say goodbye, only that we shall meet again someday. Rest in everlasting peace with our Lord God."

With that, he turned to greet several of the women in the village who were about to initiate the ritual of cleansing her body for burial. Joshua watched the women as they gently went to carry out the ritual of taharah by pouring water over her body. She was then wrapped in a simple white cloth, the final step before internment.

The procession of the entire village to the burial site, the levaya for Deborah, was a testament to their love and respect for this extraordinary but simple soul. She was buried in a simple tomb carved into the hillside. The rabbi read several prayers followed by tributes from several of the villagers. Ethan could not bring himself to speak lest he collapsed in a flood of tears. To everyone's surprise, Joshua stepped forward. He turned to the group, speaking slowly and almost in a whisper as if he were speaking to his mother.

"My mother was a pure and gentle soul in the sight of God and who dedicated her life to her family. She was a devoted wife, a true partner on life's journey. She was a loving and caring mother to her three sons. She was an example of love, compassion, duty and honor. May her life be a blessing and an example to us all as she rests in the arms of our Lord God. May God's grace be upon her."

With that, Joshua turned away and hobbled his way back to his house to his beloved garden surrounded by his flowers and birds. Seated in the garden alone, he spoke to his mother as if she were seated with him. Suddenly, everything went silent; nothing stirred; time stopped. It seemed that he was looking at her through a gossamer veil. He could see her smiling at him; her face was as radiant as the sun. At that moment, he understood and was comforted.

"Yes, I can see, Mother, you are free, happy and seated at the right hand of our Creator."

The apparition then disappeared as quickly as it came. The aroma from the flowers seemed more fragrant; the song of the birds was sweeter. He stood up and softly whispered to his mother, "It is time for me to move on, but I know you shall always be with me. Until we meet again."

In the days after the burial, Deborah's family sat Shiva, and said the Kaddish, a beautiful prayer that reflects on life, tradition and family. During the seven days of Shiva, Ethan and his three sons received condolences and an abundance of food from many of the villagers. It was both a sad and joyful week as many of her friends recollected their memories of Deborah's generosity of spirit, her quiet manner, and her simple formula for a happy life. Indeed, she had filled her niche and accomplished her life tasks. She had succeeded.

In the year after her death, Ethan fell into a deep depression over the loss of his beloved Deborah. He rarely spoke, and when he did, with tears welling, he would recall those little life moments of pure joy and happiness. Within a year, Joshua's father died. They said that the cause was a broken heart. He was buried alongside his wife of fifty years.

Soon after the burial and the attendant rituals for the dead, both his brothers, Seth and Aaron, had taken wives. Their home was extended and divided to accommodate the two new families with children soon to come. It left little room for Joshua. It became clear that these new wives found his presence disquieting. A third unmarried man sharing in the household was considered scandalous and an abomination.

And so began Joshua's first step into history…

CHAPTER 3

It was early in the morning. The sun had not cleared the hills of Galilee, but the deep purple sky was starting to give way to the first pale rays of light. The stars lingered overhead. The houses had not shed the dark shadow of the night; their occupants were still asleep. As Joshua shut the door behind him, he could feel the cool air, but it was the eerie silence that struck him. The air was perfectly still. He lingered for several long moments remembering with a mix of sadness and joy his life in the only home he had ever known. Taking a deep breath, he stepped into the stillness. As he did so, this Jewish boy could not know that he would begin a journey that would change his life and become an unsung partner in the history of Judeo-Christianity.

When the village awoke, word quickly spread that the simple and gentle man was gone. It was a sad day for many of the villagers, principally the children who had come to see him every day to sit in the garden to learn about the flowers and the fruits, and then to sing songs of praise and thanksgiving to God for His love for mankind.

He left the house with only a small pack containing some dried fruits, nuts, and several flowers from his garden to keep him company. He had never ventured beyond the shores of the Sea of Galilee. From his friend, Moshe, he had heard of a city named Jerusalem that was many miles to the south of his village, and it was here that he wanted to begin his new life. He would miss his lifelong friend who now had taken a wife, Rachel, and was raising a family. He would accept his decision to move on but not his brothers and their wives, a decision they would live to regret.

Jerusalem was the center of Judaism; it was the site of the Temple, the repository for the Ark of the Covenant that contains the Ten Commandments delivered to Moses by God. From his village, Kfar Nahum, Jerusalem lay about 72 kilometers (approx. 45 miles) to the south. He would follow the mountain trail all the way to the Holy

City. The road to Jerusalem was a long and difficult one for a man on a crutch, especially in the blistering heat of the day. His back was so painful that he had to stop several times to rest. The armpit that held the crutch was blistered and bleeding, but he pressed on despite the agonizing pain. Every painful step only reinforced his determination to reach Jerusalem. On the third day, exhausted by the heat and the exertion of walking, he found the shade of a tree alongside the road to rest and eat what was left of his meager ration of food. He had only taken a mouthful of the remaining water to wash down the unleavened bread when he saw a cart approaching very slowly. It appeared to Joshua that the cart would turn over at any minute as it was obviously overloaded. As it got closer, he could see the reason for the wobbly wagon; it was loaded with sacks of grain, melons and baskets of dates, nuts, and figs. An old man, walking alongside the straining oxen, was urging the poor beasts with curses and recriminations. Seated at the rear of the cart was a beautiful young woman whose role, it seemed, was to keep the melons from rolling off the cart. Suddenly, two rough-looking men emerged from the bush and set upon the terrified old man. When they saw the young woman cowering, they realized that they now had three very valuable prizes: the cart and oxen, the food and the woman. The thieves reckoned that these would fetch a handsome price in the market, especially the woman.

"Leave her!" Joshua called out. The two thieves turned to see a young man with a crutch hobbling toward them. They laughed at the sight of him. "You fool, this is our prize. What can a cripple like you do?" Joshua kept coming. The two bandits seeing that the man was determined and closing the distance, cursed and threatened him. "Turn around, cripple, and crawl back in the snake hole you came from or else your death will be certain."

"Let her go. I will not ask again."

"A hero, eh? Well, cripple, let us see if your bravado remains intact after we teach you to mind your own business." Their coarse laughter was cut short when Joshua met their lumbering attack with swiftness and cunning. Yes, just like a snake. He spun around in a circle, and as he did so, he raised the heavy crutch. He struck the first one with a blow to the head, leaving him in an unconscious heap. The second bandit leaped over his comrade in a rage.

"I am going to kill you, cripple, and throw you to the leopards!"

But just as quickly, Joshua dropped to the ground and jammed the end of the crutch into the thief's stomach with such force that he screamed in agony. Blood trickled from the man's mouth as he tried to utter a word. Within a moment, the man went still.

Joshua went over to the old man who was lying on the ground, severely beaten. The poor man was moaning in pain; they had broken his arm among the many bruises he had received. At the same moment, the woman came around the cart to see Joshua tending to the old man. He quickly crafted splints from branches scattered on the road and applied them to the man's arm. Joshua spoke gently, "I'm sorry for your pain, sir, but I am certain that after a while, you will completely recover." Although still in pain, the old man managed a whisper of thanks.

The woman knelt alongside Joshua as he finished fitting the splint. "Thank you, sir. You risked your life for us, complete strangers. I can't thank you enough. My uncle and I are in your debt."

Joshua replied, "No thanks are necessary. I could not stand by and allow harm come to you and your uncle." With that, Joshua stood up, "I wish you well. May God be with you." With that, he turned to leave. There were so many more miles to cover, and this little incident had left him in more pain.

"Sir, please take some rest after this encounter. You are welcome to my home. My husband and I would be honored to have you as our guest."

Joshua was tired, thirsty, and hungry, having exhausted his food supply. Worst of all, he looked more like a beggar with matted hair, unshaven and worn clothes. "I am grateful for your invitation, *Ishah* (Madame), but I am covered in dust and grime from my journey. I am not worthy to enter your home."

"I saw how you put down those bandits, and how you provided aid and comfort to my uncle. You may look like a person in distress, but I feel certain that you are more than that. Please accept my offer. We can provide you with food, clean clothes and provisions for your onward journey."

Joshua tried to remember how many days he had been walking; it all seemed to be lost in a blur from the searing heat. However, he could clearly recollect the years in his village, his mother and father, and even his heartless brothers. It was a simple life then, filled with love, beauty and friendship. He could see his lush garden, the beautiful flowers, the young children, and, of course, his only real friend, Moshe. Surely, he thought, it would do no harm to take a meal and wash. "You are very kind, *Ishah*, thank you for your offer. If it will be of no inconvenience, I would be most grateful."

"Well, it is settled then. Let us get this produce to the market that is just ahead after which we will make our way safely back to our home, and with your protection, I am certain it will be without incident. My name is Sara. And you?" Joshua was startled by the young woman's candor and directness. For a moment, he said nothing. He had never met a woman of such grace and candor. Regaining his composure, he replied simply, "Joshua".

After unloading the farm products in the market, Joshua placed the old man in the now empty cart. Sara insisted that she walk alongside him as he led the oxen. He found that Sara was not only elegant, she was also well-read and articulate. Joshua said very little. In truth, he was unable to say very much. He was fascinated as this woman kept up a steady monologue describing the farm, the season's crop, her husband, mother and father — a continuous stream that ended only when they arrived at her home.

CHAPTER 4

After a long and painful walk, they finally reached the border of the village of Shiloh, the location of the farm. As they approached the house, he quickly realized that she was no ordinary dirt farmer toiling in the heat of the desert sun. The most common form of material that was used for the construction of homes consisted of sunbaked mud bricks similar to his childhood home. This home, however, was constructed of stone, and it was larger than he had ever seen. Clearly, she was the wife of a wealthy landowner. Off to one side were the mud brick homes for the laborers who he could see tending a vast field that was resplendent with so many fruit trees and shrubs of every variety. For a brief moment, he closed his eyes, remembering the days he sat in his garden redolent with the fragrance of flowers and fruits, and of course, the birds. How long had it been since he left his home, his garden, the children and his friend, Moshe? It seemed like ages ago – another time, another place. Tears welled in his eyes. He was startled out of his reverie.

"Joshua, Joshua, are you alright? Are you in pain?" Sara asked anxiously.

"No, *Ishah*, thank you for asking. I was just thinking."

"Home?"

"Yes, home. It has just struck me; I am alone. My mother and father are gone, and there is no room for me now that my brothers have taken wives."

As they got closer, Sara's husband, Avram, came out to greet his wife. However, he noticed that his brother was not at the lead. Rather, leading the team of the lumbering oxen were his wife and a ragged-looking stranger who was hobbling on a crutch. Seeing the apprehensive look on his face, Sara assured her husband, "Hello husband, this man saved us from bandits along the road. If it weren't for him, I am certain we would not be here now."

"Thank you, sir, for your bravery and for saving the life of my brother and my wife. I am Avram. You have my gratitude. You are most welcome in our home. We shall eat and you can tell me of this unfortunate encounter."

Avram helped the old man out of the cart. He was in some pain, but managed to tell his brother, "I am indebted to him, brother. He not only saved us, he also tended to my wound."

Avram was impressed. Here was a man with a crutch that had overtaken two bandits, expertly wrapped his brother's arm and led the team of oxen a considerable distance without complaint or demand for a reward. Clearly, this was no ordinary traveler. "What is your name?" Avram asked.

"Joshua, sir."

"Well, Joshua, no doubt you must be tired and hungry. We shall prepare a feast."

Never having entered such a resplendent house, Joshua hesitated. "Thank you, sir, I am but a simple traveler covered in sand and dust; I have no clean clothes and I have not trimmed my beard. I do not wish to enter your home in this condition. I would be grateful for a meal out here."

Avram said nothing for a long time, looking into his eyes. Joshua felt as if the man was peering into his heart. Joshua broke the silence that had become uncomfortable, "Truly, sir, I would be happy to take a meal here under a tree."

At that moment, Sara emerged from the house. "Joshua, the servants have prepared a bath and clean clothes for you. Come."

Still, Joshua hesitated as the man kept up his piercing gaze. Upon hearing his wife call for Joshua, it seemed in that instant that any reservation on the part of the man disappeared. Avram nodded and smiled, "Go ahead, Joshua. She does not like to be kept waiting."

"Thank you, sir, thank you," Joshua said, grateful to be out of the man's scrutiny. Joshua took several steps toward the house, stopped and turned around to the man, and bowed, "Thank you, sir."

Joshua closed his eyes as he sat in the bath. For the first time in what seemed endless days, he felt more than a mere hungry, homeless, bedraggled itinerant. He held his breath and slid under the water. It was a moment of complete tranquility; he hadn't felt such serenity since he sat in his garden with the birds, the flowers, and his mother and father. Now it seemed that his life in his village was from another time, another place that was becoming more remote. All there was for him was the here and now. Afraid that he was taking too long in the bath, he jumped out of the water and quickly put on fresh, clean clothes. *What luxury!* He thought. He rushed from the room provided for him. With his hair dripping and still wet, he saw that his hosts were already waiting for him.

"I'm sorry if I took so long."

Sara looked at him and shook her head, smiling. At that moment, she thought that her noble hero now looked more like a wet cat. She assured him that it was no inconvenience and invited him to sit down on the plush cushions that surrounded a presentation the likes of which he had never seen before. For Joshua, the dinner could only be described as elegant. He was so hungry that it didn't matter what they served. Trying hard not to be seen as voracious, he ate slowly, as if savoring the meal. Both

Avram and Sara exchanged glances; they knew that this young man really wanted to eat enough for at least two days.

"Now, Joshua, you must tell me of your adventures. Sara tells me you are a fearless warrior who wields that crutch like a deadly weapon." Joshua reluctantly paused, eating the delicious roasted lamb. With his mouth full, he said, "Well shir, it wath really nofing." Sara giggled, and Avram frowned. Joshua took the mouthful and swallowed hard. "Sorry," he said meekly. He started, "Well sir, it was really nothing. I wouldn't describe my journey as an adventure. It was more like a forced march."

Pointing to his crutch, "This stick has been my only companion since the death of my parents. Just like my brothers, most of the people I encountered looked at me with fear and some with loathing. I heard their whispers of 'cursed, repulsive and an abomination.' They had never seen a person who was very tall, unshaven, and with shabby clothes. Because I have walked with a crutch all my life, one shoulder is higher and larger than the other. They would back away, some retreating into their homes. Although I asked, no one would offer me a cup of water.

In fact, my only companions throughout my life were the plants, flowers and trees in my garden. And there were always the birds. They taught me to sing. Our rabbi took pity on me. He was he who pulled aside the curtain of my ignorance. I took refuge in the Torah, where I discovered the relationship between God and mankind, the path in life and behaviors that constitute part of our eternal covenant with God. I'm afraid, sir, that this is the sum total of my life. The truth is that I left home not in search of riches or fame, but to find a place for myself in the world. I was on my way to Jerusalem, where I thought I might begin another path on my life's journey."

Sara was moved by the young man's rather inauspicious start in life; how sad she thought. Tears welled in her eyes. She shook her head. "Life has not been good to you, Joshua."

"On the contrary, *Ishah*, I am blessed. You and your family have welcomed me in your home, fed me and listened to my life's story. You have shown me friendship. I could not ask for more."

Avram said nothing. He listened carefully all the while stroking his ample beard. Sara noticed the gesture. It was a signal to her that her husband was thinking,…planning. Suddenly, Avram abruptly rose. "You shall stay with us for the night. We shall speak again in the morning." With that he turned to Sara, "Come, wife, let us leave Joshua. He must be tired."

Joshua propped himself up on the crutch struggling to his feet. "Thank you, sir. I am in your debt." Alone, for the moment, the silence overwhelmed him. Suddenly, he felt the full weight of his loneliness. *Truly I am alone without friend or family,* he thought. *There is no one to look after me, to care for me. Will this be my life? I despair at the thought.* He turned and hobbled to the room prepared for him. It seemed that the crutch, his leg, and the constant pain were a burden too much to bear. He sat on the cushions of his bed and cried, cried like he had not since he was a child when he was shunned by the people in the village.

Sara heard him sobbing. She had no children of her own, but she could feel the young man's pain. She began to get up to console him, but her husband, who was also awake, put a hand on her shoulder. "Leave him be, Sara. He must confront his pain alone. There is little that you can do for him, and even if you could, to what end? Will you accompany him on his journey, be a mother to him? His wounds and despair run deep. I fear that you would increase his pain and loneliness if you consoled him for a day, and then sent him on his journey. My beloved wife, your compassion and generosity of spirit are a wonder to me. Would that we all possessed your kindness. Let us discuss this in the morning."

"Yes, my dear husband, you are right," she replied, still feeling the young man's heartbreak.

The night passed slowly for Joshua. His mind was cluttered with a cascade of thoughts. Some were ugly pictures followed by beautiful scenes in his garden, and worst of all, so many feelings of grief and sadness mixed with moments of joy and happiness. Despite lying down, he could still feel the pain in his leg and back from the grueling walk from the past several days, the hunger and thirst, the rejection and the encounter on the road with the bandits, and of course, his parents. He tried to push the feelings aside but to no avail. In the end, exhaustion overcame him, and he fell into a restless sleep.

From somewhere, he could hear sounds, the sounds of people speaking, and he smelled the aroma of food being cooked. Was it a dream meant to calm his disturbing night of memories and nightmares? The speaking became louder, and the aroma more intense. He recognized the voices, and was jolted awake. He picked up his crutch and hobbled as fast as he could into the common room, stumbling in the process. "Forgive me for my tardiness," he said sheepishly.

It was Sara who spoke first, "I know that sleep did not come easily to you. I could hear you thrashing about throughout the night. I have saved some bread, olive oil, and some fruits for you. Sit, eat."

Avram said nothing as his wife fussed over the young man encouraging him to eat as if he had not eaten in days. Sadness came over him; she could not bear children after an illness that nearly claimed her life. It was one of her great regrets. Secretly, he too lamented over the years, knowing that his good fortune would not be passed on, but he never broached the subject with Sara. How could he discuss this with her? It would only add to her burden of that regret.

Sara marveled at the young man's capacity for food. The more he ate, the more she served. Joshua was so concentrated on shoveling food in his mouth, that he did not hear Avram. "Joshua?" He called twice.

Sara bent over to gesture to him that Avram was calling him. Mouth full, Joshua looked up at Avram. This time, however, he did not speak with a mouthful of bread, oil and olives.

With a little sarcasm in his voice, Avram said, "Joshua, after you have had your fill, I will show you our groves and fields."

Joshua took a hard swallow of the large mouthful, and quickly rose to his feet. "I would be honored, sir."

Avram, Sara and Joshua walked slowly, taking in the sweet fragrances of the land. This was Joshua's favorite time of the day when the sun had just emerged from the horizon. The damp air held suspended the many sweet aromas from the trees, shrubs and multitude of flowers. It was truly intoxicating for Joshua, who marveled at the abundance. As they walked, Avram pointed out the various crops and his plans to expand the farm with more fruit plantings. Sara kept up her commentaries about a variety of subjects; Joshua said nothing.

Avram noticed that Joshua said nothing, but how could he? Sara was giving them a running observation of life on the farm, the prices at the market, the dangers on the road, the haggling, and on and on. For his part, Joshua had been carefully assessing the field of crops, and the laborers tending the fields. After a lapse in Sara's commentaries, Joshua turned to Avram, "Sir, may I speak freely?"

"Yes, of course, Joshua. I welcome your thoughts."

"Thank you, sir. I would consider pruning those shrubs, and pointing to a grove of mulberry trees, planting those trees with more spacing so they get more water, and the flowers need much more attention."

"Go on," Avram was momentarily surprised by the young man's knowledge. Joshua continued without hesitation. At that moment, it was evident to Avram and Sara that this was no ordinary itinerant. Joshua's eyes sparkled with excitement, and he spoke in a torrent, pointing to a stand of orange trees, "I would advise trimming the upper branches. I'm certain that it would bear more fruit." He turned and knelt before a bed of flowers. He touched the flowers with loving tenderness. "And for these, sir, may I suggest the following…." He kept up his animated monologue, oblivious to his hosts. He was now back in his garden, speaking to the flowers and singing with the birds. He stopped as tears welled in his eyes. Sara understood. She knelt beside him and put her arms around him. "It's home, isn't it?" she asked him tenderly.

"I'm sorry. I miss home, my family, the garden and the little children. I miss my days in the synagogue."

Joshua felt a strong hand on his shoulder. Embarrassed by his account, "I'm sorry, sir." In a tone of voice that even surprised his wife, Avram gently said, "Come, let us continue our walk."

"Yes, sir."

They walked in silence for several long moments. Seeing the chief gardener, Avram motioned to him, "Nathan, this is my guest, Joshua. You will spend the next few hours with him. He has much to offer us." He then turned to Joshua, "Please share your thoughts with Nathan. At noon, you will join us." With that, Avram and Sara turned and left the two gardeners.

Joshua found that Nathan was a kindly man with a soft voice and gentle eyes. His long hair was tangled and entirely white, as was most of his beard. His skin had that leathery look after years in the sun. But to Joshua, it was the man's hands that impressed him. They were huge and gnarled; several fingers were twisted with age and accidents in the fields. "Well, my young friend, let us walk together. Show me what you said to Master Avram that impressed him so."

"Yes, sir," replied Joshua.

"Do not call me 'sir'", came the old man's terse reply. "My name is Nathan, not sir."

"Yes, sir…er, Nathan."

As they walked, Nathan and Joshua traded thoughts and experiences about attending crops and flowers. The old gardener was impressed with the young man's knowledge, and the young gardener was amazed at the wealth of understanding and practical wisdom of the old man. They spent hours together discussing fertilizing, pruning, planting and crop rotation. The bond between them was instantaneous; it would soon grow from mutual admiration to a deep and lasting friendship.

For the first time in all his years, Joshua felt a sense of companionship and belonging. Perhaps, he thought, that this is what God has ordained for me, and if so, he silently thanked the Lord for bestowing such a gift.

"Nathan, I must go now as the master of the house has summoned me," Joshua said with a little regret in his voice. Taking Nathan's hand, he said, "Thank you, I am grateful for your time and generosity." Then he took his leave and hurried to his meeting with Avram and Sara.

He had hardly crossed the threshold of the house, where Sara was waiting for him with plates full of bread, cheese, olives, grapes, figs and cakes, and Joshua's favorite: honey. "Come, Joshua, sit, eat. You must be hungry." However, Sara noticed that Joshua winced as he slowly lowered himself.

"Are you alright, son? Are you in pain?"

In that instant, Joshua forgot the pain in his back and leg. "Son," he thought, she called me son! How many years had it been since he heard that word? Son! She called me son! Tears began to well in his eyes.

Thinking that his tears were a reaction to the pain in his leg, she said so gently, "Here, let me help you." She held him as he sank to the ground. She looked about and found several cushions to ease the pain.

"Thank you, Sara. You have been so kind. Yes, I may have done too much walking." He thought to himself, *have I offended her by calling her by her name?* Sara seemed to understand the change in his reference to her. She just smiled.

Unbeknownst to both of them, Avram was watching and listening to the exchange. He heard Sara call Joshua "son". He put his finger on his pursed lips. He noticed that for the past two days, Sara had sparkled. It seemed like ages since he had seen his wife, so...happy, yes, happy. He smiled and thought that this was what motherhood must look like.

Sara was putting plates of food in front of Joshua, who was only too willing to eat whatever was put in front of him. *I don't know where my next meal will be.* She kept fluffing his pillows while keeping up a staccato stream of questions. "Did you enjoy your visit with Nathan? Did you know that he has been with us for years? Are you feeling better? Are you enjoying your stay here?" Joshua was searching for the right moment to respond.

"Yes, yes, yes, and yes," he responded between her breaths before the ensuing question. At that moment, to his great relief, Avram appeared.

"My dear wife, we must let Joshua rest. After all, he has only arrived two days ago."

"Yes, my husband, you are quite right." As she was walking away, she turned to Joshua, "You will stay with us for a while?"

Joshua was stunned. How could he refuse such a generous invitation? He looked over to Avram, waiting for a sign. He didn't have to wait too long. "You are welcome to stay. Come, Sara, let the young man eat in peace."

For the remainder of the day, he sat by himself under the shade of an olive tree. He looked around him, taking in his surrounding as if it were the first time. He saw the fruit trees, the fields of barley and wheat, the fig trees, grape vines and the sea of flowers. He could hear the music of the birds. He closed his eyes and saw in his mind what he had just seen with his eyes. It was captured as a permanent memory. He whispered, "Thank you, my Lord God, for these years. You have watched over me and have blessed me a thousand times. Wherever I go, I know that You are with me. I am not afraid of what lies before me. I put myself completely in Your Hands." He opened his eyes to see the brilliant sun as it showered rays through the trees. The flowers were ablaze with a myriad of breathtaking colors, their fragrances overpowering. "Truly, Lord, these flowers are a wonder and a testament to Your greatness! See how they have raised their faces up to Heaven, giving glory to You."

Sara saw him standing alone in front of a particularly beautiful patch of daisies whose stark white leaves and rich golden center held him almost hypnotically. His contemplation was interrupted, "Joshua, my husband would like to see you. Will you join us for dinner?"

"Yes, of course. Thank you." It was not the invitation that impressed him; it was the tone of her voice. It was not the tone of the gracious host. It was reminiscent of a voice he had heard so many years before. The voice of the woman who nursed him, cared for him, and taught him love and compassion.

"Good, shall we go then?" Sara then stepped forward and put her arm firmly under Joshua's free arm. He felt a sudden rush of joy. He looked over to Sara, and smiled at her as she began a litany of the dinner menu. He could feel her warmth; it radiated like the sun. It was the warmth that only a mother could convey.

It was more than a dinner; it was truly a feast. As he entered the dining room, he caught his breath. Candles gave the room a festive air. The table was covered with an astonishing array of fruits, vegetable, and bread. The air was redolent with the aroma of roasted lamb. The sight and smells were overwhelming for Joshua. He had never seen such a spectacle. Sensing his confusion, Sara said, "Joshua, it is Purim! Today we celebrate Esther, Queen of Persia, who saved the Jewish people from execution by Haman." Joshua had lost track of time during his lonely trek. But in a moment, it all came back to him. Yes, of course, Purim. He recalled the happy days in the village when the children and adults celebrated with song and dance, and copious amounts of wine. "Happy Purim," he said to Sara and Avram, the traditional greeting for that day.

"Sit, sit," Sara urged. Joshua remained standing until Avram was seated in recognition of Avram's position as head of the house. Once again, Sara helped Joshua to sit. Avram watched with a combination of pleasure and amusement as Sara smothered the young man in an avalanche of maternal care. Avram raised a cup of wine and wished his wife and Joshua a happy Purim. With that, the feast began in earnest.

Sara suddenly exclaimed, "Oh, I almost forgot." She bolted from the room. Joshua looked at Avram questioningly, but Avram merely shrugged. "My beloved wife is like a bird. She is in constant motion. It is difficult to keep up with her. Her energy is boundless. I am certain we will be surprised when she returns."

Just then, Sara emerged, holding a small clay pot. She sat down and placed the pot in front of Joshua. "It is honey, your favorite," she said softly. Joshua was at a loss for words; Avram closed his eyes and shook his head in a sign of resignation. "Do you see, Joshua, what I mean?"

Joshua reached over to Sara, gently took her hand and kissed it. With a trembling voice and a tear, "Thank you, Sara, thank you."

Dinner lasted long into the evening. When it seemed that there was no more food to consume, Sara brought out more. Joshua thought there must be some inexhaustible supply somewhere. With Sara leading, they sang traditional Purim songs with Avram and Joshua trying but failing to stay on key: "Utzu Eitzah" and "U Mordechai Yatza", and as was the biblical command: celebrate these days as days of drinking and rejoicing". And so they did. And then to Joshua's surprise, Avram rose to his feet and began to sing and dance. There was no particular routine to his dancing, just joyful movement propelled by copious amounts of wine. Sara bounced up, and she, too, in no particular style, began to swing her arms and twirled round and round. Joshua watched in amazement and joy. He clapped his hands not to any tempo, but to express his enjoyment of the moment in the only way he could. Yes, it was the most joyful Purim celebration.

As the festivities came to an end, an exhausted and inebriated Avram collapsed on to the floor in heaps of laughter. Sara was a naturally ebullient person without much need for wine. She quickly regained her composure, and said to her husband, "My dear husband, our celebration has come to an end, but we must share this abundance, including the wine, with the farm workers, for surely they do not enjoy the same bounty." She turned to Joshua, "Would you help me to deliver this food and wine to the laborers who should also be able to celebrate as we have with the same abundance."

Sara and Joshua loaded the dinner, wine and sweets in two large baskets and carried them to Nathan's cottage, where they were greeted by several of the workers who were also celebrating the holiday. The guests quickly unloaded the baskets; the women took the food, while the men took the wine. Nathan and his wife, Deborah, extended their Purim wishes and offered their gratitude to Sara for her generosity, "Thank you, Sara. You have made this day even more special." Nathan invited both Sara and Joshua to join their Purim celebrations. Sara gently demurred, "I am afraid I must return to tend to my husband who has celebrated the holiday well beyond his capacity to stand." That prompted laughter from the others. "However, I am certain that Joshua would enjoy another Purim celebration."

"Yes, yes!" Nathan exclaimed. "Please, Joshua, I am certain that our guests would like to meet so young a master gardener." Joshua could not decline; Sara had thrown him into a tender and welcome trap. Not wishing to offend his new dinner host, Joshua replied, "Thank you, Nathan, I would be pleased to celebrate this holiday with you. Happy Purim!"

It was well into the early morning hours that Joshua hobbled, or rather stumbled, to his quarters, not so much from his wilted leg, but from having drunk too much wine, and consumed more food than he had ever had in his life. He fell into his bed face first, and did not move until late in the morning when Sara woke him. She was concerned about his absence from breakfast until he turned over. She repressed a laugh. "Goodness, son, you look rather rough. I assume the Purim festival was a success."

For his part, all that Joshua could do was mumble something about never, ever, doing such a thing again for the remainder of his life. Sara managed to help him to his feet, and together they stumbled outside to sit under a tree. Avram was long gone to work with the laborers. Sara thought better than to offer Joshua any more food or drink for fear of the consequences of an unsettled stomach. For the longest time, he could hardly string two words together, muttering something about pains in his head and stomach. They sat there for a long time; neither spoke. Then it happened: a moment that Sara would never forget for the remainder of her life. Joshua slowly rested his head on Sara's shoulder and fell sound asleep. Tears of joy welled in Sara's eyes. It was an experience that she thought she would never have. She put her arm around Joshua, who stirred for a moment and then settled himself more comfortably on her shoulder.

Sara did not know how long she sat there with Joshua fast asleep on her shoulder, but for Sara, the time passed too quickly. She heard Avram calling her name; Joshua startled awake upon hearing Avram's voice, and he bolted upright. "I'm sorry, Sara, I didn't mean to…."

Sara interrupted him, "It is I who should thank you."

Joshua looked at her quizzically. He thought, why should she thank me? Before he was about to ask Sara what she meant, Avram appeared. "Ah, there you are, my dear wife. I have been looking for you. And Joshua, I understand from Nathan that you thoroughly enjoyed yourself judging by the amount of wine he said you consumed."

Joshua rose, still unsteady on his feet, and sheepishly replied, "I am sorry, sir. I won't let that happen again."

Avram chuckled, "Hmm, when I was your age, I said the same thing…until I did it again."

When they arrived at the house, Avram took a large cup of wine. He gestured to Joshua to offer a sip. Joshua turned a ghostly white and demurred. Sara looked at the poor young man sympathetically; Avram smiled wryly. Although Sara produced her usual abundant dinner, Joshua ate only a few morsels. During the meal, it occurred to Joshua that he had almost forgotten about his journey to Jerusalem; he felt at home here and had lost a sense of time. He said to both Sara and Avram, "You both have been very kind and generous to me, but I do not wish to overstay my welcome. I will take my leave tomorrow."

Sara looked over to Avram. Avram slowly nodded. Although not a word passed between them, it became clear to Joshua that they were sharing the same unspoken thought.

Avram was a strong man who had toiled his entire life on this farm that was passed to him by his father. It was a good life, but a hard one. He was blessed with an adoring wife, an equal partner in life, and a comfortable life for both of them. Although not a particularly religious man, he silently thanked God for his good fortune. And yet, there was something missing: an heir. Sara had felt the pain of guilt for their childless marriage, but bore it silently. However, Avram, for as hard a man as he was, his heart ached for Sara. He saw how she had enjoyed caring for Joshua in a maternal way. He would not deny her this special moment to announce their plan. He nodded to Sara, "My dear Sara, you should do the honors."

For a moment, Sara was at a loss for words. She looked over to Avram again for approval. Avram merely nodded. In the meantime, Joshua was becoming increasingly anxious. *What are they going to say?* he thought.

Overwhelmed with emotion, Sara reached over to Joshua, took his hand, and simply said, "We would like you to stay."

Joshua was speechless. For several long moments, he said nothing. What could he say? Thank you? You're too kind? Words seemed so inadequate. As he struggled to find the right words, a look of sadness came over her. She thought perhaps he didn't want to stay. Joshua then let go of her hand, and threw his arms around Sara, and in a moment of sheer joy, he blurted, "Yes, yes, I would very much like to stay."

Joshua had found a home; Sara had found the child she always wanted. Avram saw the look on Sara's face, and it warmed his heart. He had done the right thing for her. As for Joshua, he realized that the young man was clearly no ordinary person. He was intelligent, articulate and knowledgeable, especially about plants, trees and shrubs. Above all, he was a gentle young man, serious and sincere. He demonstrated respect for the workers and an ability to communicate with them on equal terms. Beyond all that, and most importantly, he saw Joshua's respect and care for Sara.

CHAPTER 5

For Avram, this was a pivotal moment in his life. He closed his eyes for a few seconds as if he was mentally ratifying his decision. His voice was solemn; his words came slowly, "Joshua, you have demonstrated that you are a person of intelligence, integrity and compassion. I have seen the way you treat those who are less fortunate and who must labor day and night for survival. I am no longer the young man that I was. My brother is too old to be leading the cart; and I do not want to put my beloved Sara at risk of harm or worse on the road. I need help with managing this farm for our benefit and for the loyal workers who have given their lives to grow this farm. I am now entrusting you with that role. Henceforth, you shall administer this farm, manage the workers and take our produce to market. Sara will continue to manage the finances. Her skills with the accounts are unmatched."

"Sir, I don't deserve such an honor. But for your generosity, sir, I am but a mere peasant. Surely, you could find someone more worthy."

Avram responded, "You just confirmed my decision. Now, let us take dinner and celebrate this important day."

It was done. Joshua was stunned. Can I do this? Do I have the skills, and the temperament to manage workers who are older and more experienced than I? What if I fail? On and on, he ran the questions in his mind in a dizzying circle.

Sara was ecstatic. Joshua was here to stay! Now, every day she could care for him as her own. He was still a young man, and clearly for Sara, he was still in need of loving parents, especially a loving mother. In her mind, she planned how she would go about looking after him: new clothes, a more comfortable bed, regular hair trimming and, of course, preparing his favorite meals even though he ate everything put in front of him.

Dinner was a sumptuous affair that included beer this time. Avram did not particularly like beer, but tolerated it because Sara thought beer would be better for Joshua's digestion. She watched with smiling satisfaction as Joshua ate as if it were going to be his last meal. Yes, this was one of the most important aspects of her role of what a mother should do for her son: feed him. It also helped that Joshua continued to compliment Sara's cooking with his every forkful. The meal ended too soon for Sara when Avram declared, "Let us get some rest. We have much to do, Joshua."

Joshua was so excited that sleep would not come. His mind was cluttered with questions, tasks, and all the events of the next day. There was so much to learn. Had he made a mistake? Should he take his leave before anyone depended on him? What if the workers object? The questions kept coming until exhaustion overtook him.

"Joshua, wake up! Avram is waiting for you for breakfast," Sara said softly. Joshua stirred, and seeing Sara standing there unnerved him. *The first day and I am already late,* he thought.

"I'm so sorry, Sara. I only went to sleep when daylight was coming through the window," Joshua replied, jumping up from his bed. Clad only in his bedclothes, he rushed into the dining room. Clearly, Avram was not pleased. Not an auspicious start to his new role, Joshua thought. "I'm so sorry, sir. I …"

Avram interrupted, "The first order of business today is for you to get out of your bedclothes."

"Yes, sir, yes, of course," Joshua replied as he ran back into his bedroom. As he was pulling off his clothes, searching for his sandals, he could not hear Sara and Avram laughing. Joshua sheepishly re-entered the dining room, "I'm so sorry, sir. It won't happen again."

Avram's stern face belied his true feeling. "Well, if you are ready, Joshua," Avram said with feigned sarcasm. The pair walked over to the common area where the laborers were already waiting for Avram and the "new young master". As they approached the circle of men, their whispers and grumbles ceased.

"We shall be meeting with Nathan and the other workers to inform them of my decision for you to take over your role as the farm manager. Beware, Joshua, these are hard men who have spent their lives in the fields. Their skills as farmers are impressive, skills that have been passed down from one generation to another. They will not take kindly to a young man whom they do not know and to whom they will now answer. You will need to earn their respect both as an administrator and as a farmer with skills equal to or better than theirs."

Before Joshua could utter a feeble reply, they entered the room's center, where the men were sitting in a circle. Immediately, all the men rose to their feet. "*Shalom Aleichem*" was the greeting from all the men. Avram acknowledged the greeting, "Peace upon you." All eyes turned to Joshua. With a bow of his head, which the men silently understood that the gesture was one of respect, Joshua said simply but confidently, "*Shalom Aleichem.*" A first good step, thought Avram.

Avram then beckoned the men to sit. They listened quietly as Avram announced his decision to appoint Joshua as the new farm manager. "You will show him the same courtesy and respect that you have shown me over these years. I trust this young man. He has demonstrated to me his considerable skills, and most importantly his commitment to work for the benefit of all of us." He then turned to Joshua.

For several long moments, Joshua, with his head bowed, said nothing. Unaccustomed to such an exhibition, Avram and the men looked at one another questioningly. There was an uneasy silence. Is this our new manager? They thought. Then, Joshua looked up and straightened himself. Whether by magic or miracle, he seemed transformed. He was no longer the young intruder they had seen earlier. He looked directly at each man in the group; there was an unmistakable confidence in his voice, "I promise you my total commitment to this farm and to each of you and your families. You have much to teach me, and I will hopefully make a small contribution. We shall succeed together." There was a stunned silence; Avram was speechless.

Without waiting for a signal from Avram, Joshua leaned on his crutch and started to walk. Again, with a bow of his head, he said, "Shalom, shalom." He turned and left. Avram remained with the men. Joshua met Sara at the door. She must have been waiting for news of the meeting from Avram, but instead, here was Joshua. Sara noticed it instantly. Despite his condition, there was a change in his stature. Here was a poised and self-assured young man in front of her. He took her hand, "Thank you, Sara, for everything you have done for me. It has been a long time since I felt the tenderness of a loving mother." He then quickly added, "But may I please have breakfast now? I'm starving!"

With tears of joy in her eyes, she put her arm around his waist. "Of course, my son. I have already prepared it for you."

CHAPTER 6

Joshua threw himself into his new role. He met regularly with the group and then privately with each worker and his respective family. It soon became clear to the workers and their families that the new manager was more than just an administrator; he was a unique young man. The workers agreed that he was very knowledgeable about farming, planting, pruning and crop rotation. Under his supervision, the fields of barley and wheat, the fig trees and grape vines flourished, producing an exceptionally large crop. However, they also learned that he was a scholar who had studied the Torah. To the delight of the women, they found that he was also an excellent cook, which was not met with much favor by the men. However, several men agreed, albeit secretly, that he was a better cook than their wives. As happened in his home village, children were particularly drawn to him. When not supervising, he would keep them captivated by his adventures as a boy as well as with Bible stories. They especially enjoyed playing with him. Their favorites were "Three Sticks" (where sticks are spaced at ever-increasing distances. Children would jump between the sticks trying not to step on one) and throwing a ball. Joshua was quite adept at both; the children were amazed at his skill at both of these games, and especially delighted watching him using his crutch as a lever for the jumps and for batting the ball again with his crutch.

Before long, the laborers agreed that Joshua was more than a competent farm manager: he was also a warm, compassionate, and kind human being. He was also a good listener, and despite his youth, many sought him out for advice on personal and family matters. He was conversant on many other subjects that fascinated each person on the farm. Consequently, he was a regular dinner guest of the workers' families. Here the food was simple compared to the sumptuous dinners at his home with Sara and Avram, but he made his hosts feel comfortable, praising the cooking, and engaging in conversation with them on equal terms. Those conversations were spirited, often with each member of the family offering their opinions all at the same time. Dinners were special affairs for both Joshua and the respective family. He brought warmth and laughter into each household. Without consciously realizing it, the workers and their families were drawing closer to each other, more like an extended family with Joshua as the center and binding force.

Two years passed quickly for Joshua. His relationship with Sara and Avram grew closer; he came to recognize them as his surrogate parents. He was no longer just the farm manager to Avram and a house guest to Sara. She showered him with love and endless attention to his every need. He no longer dressed like an itinerant, but as a gentleman farmer, except, however, that he took great pains not to separate himself from the workers either in dress or manner. Under Joshua's supervision, the farm flourished not only as an agricultural endeavor but also with a growing sense of community invested in the success of the farm. Sara agreed that the workers should share in the good fortune with a rise in pay and an increased allotment of the harvest. Religious feasts were now celebrated as a large family, with Avram as the elder and Sara as mother to all. For those celebrations, all the women led by Sara would join together to cook for the families; the men gathered wood for a fire, filled jars with wine and helped to roast the lamb. After dinner, everyone gathered to sing, dance and listen to stories of Abraham, Isaiah, Moses and the Exodus of the Jewish people from Egypt.

Under Joshua, the farm was transformed. It was no longer about master and servant, but as partners in an endeavor. The farm's success came to the attention of many in the surrounding hills and valleys, so much so that it was no longer necessary for Joshua to bring the bountiful harvest to market. People from surrounding villages came directly to the farm to purchase their produce! Some arrived on foot, some came in carts to purchase a large quantity of products sufficient for a small village. Nathan and his wife, Deborah, were put in charge of this on-site market. He had become too old to manage the growing number of laborers, but given his knowledge of the farm and its produce, he and Deborah were the logical choice. Deborah was just as happy to have her husband by her side after so many years away in the fields. Nathan proved to be an excellent salesman; Deborah was adept at keeping an account of the day's takings. She and Sara had become the financial managers of the farm, much to the relief of Joshua and Avram, who were now faced with the responsibility of a farm that was growing beyond their expectations.

Joshua had negotiated the purchase of several adjacent properties, one of which was dedicated to groves of lemons, olives, grapes and figs; another was set aside for wheat and barley. Joshua had also reserved a large plot where he grew flowers of all varieties, an explosion of colors and intoxicating fragrances. To his delight, many of the workers and their families visited the tranquil garden.

The garden was also a place where he could retreat for moments of silent reflection and prayer. He found himself devoting more time to visiting his garden paradise. Occasionally, his silence was interrupted by Sara, who sought him not only to call him for dinner but also to join her son in his refuge. She sat beside him on the bench and held his hand. In those few precious moments, Joshua felt a growing and enduring love for his surrogate mother. He looked at her, quietly admiring the flowers, not wanting to disturb her. He understood and smiled. He suddenly raised her hand and kissed it. Sara was stunned as he simply said, "I love you, Mother."

CHAPTER 7

Joshua witnessed the enormous changes that had occurred since he arrived two years ago. Indeed, he was the architect of those changes. Additional workers were hired with the expansion of the farm and its produce. He witnessed births and deaths, family disputes, troubled marriages, and a growing interest in the Bible and its precepts, admonitions and the history of the Jewish people. He appointed several assistant managers that gave him more time to spend with the children and in his flowery retreat. For every member of the farm, it felt like Joshua had always been there; he had become the heart and soul of the farm.

From the growing number of people visiting the farm to purchase produce, Joshua learned of an itinerant preacher from Nazareth who had acquired a significant following. His name, they said, was Jesus and his message was of God's mercy and love, of justice and caring for the poor. From the workers, he had heard of the miracles the preacher had performed: healing the sick, curing the blind, feeding a multitude of his followers from a small basket of bread and fish, and then the most magnificent and terrifying of all these wonders, raising one from the dead. He couldn't explain why, but he found himself increasingly thinking about this Jesus of Nazareth, his message and his growing ministry. On those times when he sat meditating in his garden, or at night lying in his bed, Joshua imagined what he must be like. He couldn't get this miracle worker out of his mind. Early one morning, before the workday began, one of the farmers came to him. "Joshua, I have heard that the man, Jesus, will be passing through the village of Sychar, 15 kilometers to the north."

It was then that Joshua realized that he had to see this Jesus for himself. During dinner, Joshua spoke enthusiastically of Jesus of Nazareth with Sara and Avram, who listened quietly. He realized that only he had been speaking. "I'm sorry. I have not given you a chance to speak."

Sara spoke first, "Yes, we too have heard of this man. He has attracted many followers with his message of love and peace." She looked over to Avram, who shook his head and said nothing; but she knew what he was thinking. With the wisdom possessed only by a mother and wife, she first turned, "Joshua, I take it by your excitement that you would like to see him." She turned to Avram, knowing what he was about to say. Avram first looked at Sara and then turned to Joshua, "Do you wish to leave to join this Jesus?"

"Oh, no sir, I would never leave you and Mother. I have heard so much that I would like to see this man for myself. It will only be a few days, sir. With your permission, of course."

Satisfied, Avram nodded slowly, "Very well, Joshua, go."

Sara smiled knowingly. Joshua replied, "Thank you, sir, thank you."

On the morning of his departure, several of the men and women met him to wish him well on his journey. Sara had prepared a large quantity of food and water. Several of the wives of the workers had also prepared his favorite foods for his journey. Joshua was overwhelmed by this outpouring of love and kindness. He was also overwhelmed by the weight of these gifts.

"Thank you, Mother; thank you, my dear friends. I am certain that this abundance will carry me for my journey."

One of the wives stepped forward, "Joshua, go with God. We hope your encounter with this Jesus of Nazareth will fulfill your search."

Joshua was momentarily startled by her remark. But then, it had become common knowledge that Joshua was an unsettled soul who needed to discover his own path wherever that took him. This meeting with Jesus might help him to begin that journey. Avram stepped forward and said, "Go with my blessing. We await your return."

Joshua bowed his head, "Thank you, sir." He was about to turn to leave but then turned to Sara, who was trying to hold back her tears. Joshua took her hand and kissed it. "Thank you, Mother. I will miss you," and addressing the group, "I will return soon."

Joshua covered the mountainous 15 kilometers in two days. On the evening of the first night, as he lay on his blanket, he marveled at the black sky with a breathtaking array of stars like tiny diamonds scattered in the heavens, complemented by a full moon that cast a silver shower over the land. Its enormity struck him. He felt small and overawed. What are we in the face of such magnificence? Who but God could have created this splendor? With the beauty of the expanse above him and the excitement of meeting Jesus, he could not sleep. He kept rolling these thoughts in his restless mind: In the unlikely event he did have an opportunity to speak to this Jesus, what would he say? *He had performed miracles, fed thousands and preached love and peace. Why would he speak to me? I am a mere farmer; I tend fields, trees and flowers; I am not worthy of such an honor. It is arrogance for me to believe that he would stop to speak to me. He is leading hundreds, maybe thousands of followers.* Joshua decided that it would be enough if Jesus merely looked in his direction. He finally fell into a half-sleep as the daylight began its passage over the eastern hills bringing another day of brutal heat.

He was startled awake by the sound of several travelers. He quickly raised himself to his elbow, uneasy until he heard one say, "Shalom". Joshua took hold of his crutch and stood up. Putting his right hand over his heart, he replied, "Shalom". The man, who was about the same age as Joshua, replied, "I am Binyamin and this is my wife, Ester. These are my children. We have come from Jericho to see the preacher they call Jesus and to hear his message."

Joshua replied, "I am Joshua, and I too am on a similar journey."

"We have been traveling for three days. We need to reach the next village so that my wife who is with child and my children may rest. They have been without food for a day, and our water is all but gone." Benyamin himself looked exhausted.

Joshua replied, "Benyamin, you and your family are welcome to share my provisions. Please sit and let us break bread together." He then opened his sack and offered bread, fig, dates, olives and cheese to Benyamin who, in turn, distributed the food first to his wife and then to his children. After the meal, Benyamin offered a brief prayer of thanksgiving.

"Bless you, Joshua, for your kindness and generosity. You are welcome to continue your journey with us."

"Thank you, Benyamin. You are too kind. I fear that my crutch and I would slow your progress. I wish you a safe journey." Benyamin was about to leave when Joshua bundled a large part of his food and water in a sack and gave it to him. "You and your family will need this more than I."

Joshua watched them walk away until they disappeared behind a hill and were gone. He then packed the remainder of his food and water and began the next leg of his journey. It would take another full day for him to reach the city of Sychar, located in Samaria at the foothills of Mount Ebal. The city was well known as the place near where Jacob's well was located. It was dark when he entered the city. There were no firelights – just a peaceful silence. He found a spot under an olive tree where he spent the night in anticipation of seeing the preacher that so many have spoken about. Joshua was awakened by the sound of the city waking and preparing for the day's commerce. He asked a passerby whether he had heard the news that the preacher was going to pass on a road near the city.

"Yes, we have heard. Some have dared to say that he is the Messiah, as foretold in the Bible. Others say his message does not contradict the prophets; it is a message of peace and love for our fellow man. There will be those in this city that will line the road to see him for themselves. Others will not wish to oppose the rabbis. Each must make his own decision. And you sir?" Pointing to Joshua's crutch, he said, "Are you here to be cured of your condition?"

"No, sir, I only wish to witness him for myself. I have heard of the miracles, but I was born with this 'condition' as you say. It was God's will and I accept it as such."

The man felt chided by Joshua's reply. "I mean you no offense, sir. I have heard that many flock to this man only just for a cure."

Joshua replied, "No offense taken. Do you have any idea when he might arrive?"

"No, but it must be soon because there are already many people who have passed here to get a glimpse of him." The man turned to walk away. He stopped, turned around to face Joshua, "I wish you well in your quest. Shalom, shalom."

CHAPTER 8

Joshua sat under the mulberry tree until he saw a large group of people walking past him. The group's leader saw Joshua but did not recognize him as part of his entourage. He said, "Are you here, sir, to witness the prophet Jesus?"

They are calling him a prophet, Joshua thought. "Yes, sir, I am. Do you know when he will arrive?"

The leader of the group responded, "He and his followers left Ephraim earlier today and are presently resting at Jacob's well. They will pass on the road between Mount Ebal and Mount Gerizim. The well is barely three kilometers away southwest of Sychar. Make haste, he will pass through there very soon."

"Thank you, sir." With that, Joshua raised himself and threw the sack over his shoulder. Despite the pain from the long journey, he put the crutch under his arm and set off. He had not come this far only to miss this preacher. He did not need directions; he had only to follow the long line of people. In the distance, he could see the slope of the land rise that led to where he had to go. As he made his way, numerous other travelers passed him. He could hear their cruel whispers, "Look at that poor man hobbling as fast as his crutch will take him. It's so funny to see him bouncing along like a frog." Another passed him, putting as much distance between him and Joshua as if he were a leper. "This vagrant must also be looking for a miracle. There are so many people afflicted with disease, deformities and disfigurements. They should all be put away from view. It's disgusting."

As the hill became steeper, Joshua began to struggle. He was breathing heavily and the pain in his back was excruciating. The path was littered with potholes, stones and broken branches. Joshua was so intent on reaching the summit of the hills that he did not notice the rut. It was not deep; a non-handicapped person could easily walk over it. His crutch dug into the rut. His forward motion made his fall that much harder. He fell face forward, striking his head on a large stone. His world went black.

He wasn't certain how long he had been unconscious. He awoke with a fierce pain in his head and blood running down his face. His knees were scraped and bleeding. He lay there for a long while, trying to grasp what had happened. He shook his head, trying to adjust his focus. As he became more aware of his surroundings, he raised himself to his right knee and felt pains in his left shoulder, the crutch shoulder, and ribs. He was covered in dirt and blood. He could see the other travelers walking around him, avoiding him as if he were some hapless tramp who had come to grief. No one stopped to offer him help.

He had to stand up; he had to, otherwise he would miss the preacher. He naturally reached out to get his crutch, but it was gone. *My crutch, where is it?* Suddenly, he felt a panic rush over him. He turned left, then right; he crabbed around to see if it was behind him. *Where is it? Did someone take it? Was it broken, and now a part of the trash that littered the path?* He was overcome with horror; he lowered his head and began to cry. He had come so far only to be thwarted by a fall. But then, to his surprise, he heard, "Sir, sir, is this yours?" He lifted his head.

Standing in front of him was a little boy holding his crutch that was taller than he was. He reached for it and held it in his arms in a loving embrace. The little boy turned to catch up to his parents. With tears in his eyes, Joshua called out, "Thank you, thank you." The boy turned, smiled and waved to him, and then disappeared in the thick of the crowd.

It was only when he raised himself, did he see and feel the extent of his injuries. However, the only thing that mattered was that he reached the main road where the preacher would be passing. He wiped the blood from his face with his sleeve and dusted himself off. Putting the crutch under his left arm was agonizing. He took a deep breath through gritted teeth and took a first step. He cried out with pain. Each step was an excruciating effort. His face was distorted with pain. With each step, he repeated aloud, "I have to get to the top, I have to get to the top."

He looked up to see how close he was to the road. It couldn't be more than about 60 cubits (approx. 15 feet). *Almost there, keep going.* His head was throbbing and the cuts and bruises were raw, but he would not be deterred. He saw that there was a large crowd already lining the road. He struggled the last few feet, and then, at last, he was there! *I made it!* As he got to the side of the road, people who saw him, and saw his wretched condition quickly distanced themselves from him as if he had a sickness. He heard someone say, "Move away, he must be diseased." He was so excited that he forgot the pain and the harsh words.

"Look, there they are," Joshua heard. In the distance, he could see a mass of people in a slow procession. The excitement in the crowd was like electricity; Joshua could feel it as well. And then, after several long and anxious minutes, the first person in the procession cleared the rise in the road. There he was, the preacher! As the man leading the company got closer, an extraordinary thing happened: rather than raising their voices in praise, which is what Joshua expected, the bystanders suddenly went quiet. What earlier was expectant excitement had become a blanket of silence. At long last, he was going to see the man who was being hailed as a prophet, a healer, a champion of the poor and oppressed.

The man they called Jesus of Nazareth was coming closer to where Joshua was standing. Up until that moment, Joshua was expecting an elegantly dressed patriarchal figure with an entourage that was equally grand. But to his amazement, this celebrated person was holding a gnarled staff, and was dressed more like a pauper than a revered preacher. His skin was deeply tanned because of the long way he had made under the brutal desert sun; his hair was long; his beard was straggly, and his sandals were worn.

Off to his right, Joshua saw an old woman in ragged clothes on her hands and knees. As Jesus was passing, she began to cry out, "Lord, Lord, help me!" She continued to shout, "Merciful Lord, Son of God, have pity on me!" One of his followers attempted to silence her, "Stay away, woman, my master has no time for the likes of you!" But she shouted all the louder, "Lord, Lord, have pity on me!" Jesus turned to the follower and said, "Why do you cast her aside? Is she not one of God's children? She has professed her belief in the Son of God." The poor woman scrabbled to the feet of Jesus, and touched the hem of his robe. At that instant, she exclaimed, "I can see! My Lord

God, I can see!" He reached down and helped her to her feet. The prophet turned to the crowd following him, "Those who believe in me shall be rewarded by my Father with eternal salvation." She joined his followers, proclaiming that he was the Son of God.

Joshua, along with everyone else standing on the roadside, saw the miracle and heard the words of Jesus. Several of the bystanders began exclaiming, "Hosha na, hosha na!" The Prophet walked a few more yards. Suddenly, Jesus stopped in front of Joshua. He looked directly at Joshua who could now see his eyes. They were dark as coals, and at first glance, seemed fierce. Joshua felt as if they were burning a hole in him. Overwhelmed by his nearness, Joshua nearly staggered. At first, Joshua was frightened, but then he began to feel an overwhelming sense of tranquility come over him.

Given his disability, he could not kneel in the face of a man such as this, but he tried, and fell over. There were those around that began to laugh at Joshua's gesture of respect. Jesus turned to them, and said, "This man deserves your praise – not your scorn."

"What is your name?" the preacher asked, as he gently helped the young man to his feet.

Trembling, "Joshua, sir," was all that he could manage.

A gentle smile crossed the preacher's face, not fierce at all, his eyes were gentle. His hand touched Joshua's face, and in that instant, the bleeding and headache instantly stopped. He felt as if he had been struck by lightning. He started to shudder. The preacher then put his hands on his shoulders, whereupon the excruciating pain he felt from his fall instantly disappeared. He continued to look at him.

"We will meet again, Joshua."

With that, Jesus turned and continued his journey, with the crowd following closely behind. He watched the preacher until he disappeared in the distance. The crowd of onlookers quickly dispersed. Many expressed disappointment because initially, like Joshua, they were expecting something very different. Perhaps, they thought that they would be overwhelmed by a radiating presence surrounded by angels that commanded awe and fear, certainly not someone who looked like them. "Why, he was just a commoner, a simple Jew, not unlike us; certainly not the Son of God, the Messiah that was prophesized," they said.

It was suddenly very quiet. Joshua remained as if he were frozen in place. He found himself alone on the roadside. It was then that he realized what had just happened. All his cuts and bruises had disappeared! His shoulder was no longer painful. He felt his head; there was no blood; and his shoulder could hold the crutch. Was this a miracle?

CHAPTER 9

It took several long days retracing his steps along the mountain path before he would reach his home. The heat was blistering, forcing Joshua to rest repeatedly, but despite the heat, all he could think about was the encounter with the man, Jesus. *What did he mean when he said, "We will meet again, Joshua?"* He played the scene of his encounter with the prophet over and over in his mind. And then there were his injuries and the pain – they were gone! *How could that be?*

He walked through the well-worn paths encountering wealthy merchants in their carriages, travelers and beggars. On the evening of the third day, he came upon a small, nameless settlement. As Joshua hobbled passed the rough mud-brick shelters, he could feel the eyes of fear and suspicion. They looked at Joshua with disdain, fearful of anyone with a handicap. Ordinarily, Joshua would avoid their eyes and continue on his way, but thirst and hunger forced him to stop. He saw two women drawing water from a well. He approached them and asked, "May I trouble you for a cup of water?" The first woman looked horrified at the sight of the ragged man on crutches and hastily turned away. The second woman could see that the hobbling man was in a desperate way. His clothes were disheveled and covered in dust. The look on his face told her that the man was not threatening – just thirsty and hungry. She took a cup of water and handed it to Joshua who gulped it down without stopping to catch his breath. He held out the cup and looked at her. She understood. She filled the cup again and passed it to him.

"Thank you, *ishah*, thank you."

"Looking at you, I imagine you are also hungry. Wait here." Without waiting for his reply, the young woman retreated into one of the shelters. After several long minutes, she returned with a wooden plate filled with dried fruit, olives, and bread. "This is all that I can provide. We are very poor," she said almost apologetically as she handed him the plate.

"Thank you, *ishah*. You are not poor, you are rich in compassion, kindness and generosity," Joshua replied as he shook his head. Pointing to the plate in front of him, he said, "This is wealth beyond the fortunes of kings."

As he hungrily dug into the food, the young woman asked Joshua, "Where are you going? The nearest village from here is miles away, and the road can be dangerous. And worse than the distance and danger, you will be traveling in the brutal heat. You must be a determined man to risk such a journey."

Joshua closed his eyes as if recalling the image, "I came to see the prophet they call Jesus. I am now returning to my home in Shiloh."

"Yes, I have heard the same from many travelers who passed through here. Did you see him? What was he like? Is it possible for me to see him? she asked.

Joshua was searching for a response, "He looks no different than you or I – a simple man, yet with a simple but powerful message. I do not have words; it was both frightening and serene at the same time."

They were silent for a long while. What more could he say? Then he pulled himself up and with a bow of his head, he said, "Thank you, *ishah*, I will remember you in my prayers."

Embarrassed by his remark, she replied softly, "Thank you, sir. May I ask your name?"

Joshua smiled, "I am certainly no 'sir', I am merely Joshua. And you, what are you called?"

"Avigail, my name is Avigail," she replied.

"Well, Avigail, I must be off. I still have many miles to travel. Once again, thank you. May God bless you." With that, Joshua turned and began to walk away.

"Joshua, will you return this way? If you do, I will make a feast for you," she blurted. Avigail thought, *he is no ordinary man. Something tells me that I will see him again.* A strange feeling had overcome her, she felt… yes, happy at the encounter; no not happy, but tranquil.

"Perhaps, Avigail, perhaps I will, but a feast is not necessary. Your kindness is more than enough. Our God to whom I look for my future will determine my path."

With that, he stepped onto the path and limped away, but before turning a bend in the road, Joshua turned around to see her standing watching him. He gave a wave, and then he was gone. When she went into her house, her sister looked at her and said, "What happened to you sister? You look different."

CHAPTER 10

It was another several grueling days until he reached Shiloh and home. Although the previous days had been eventful and exhausting, returning home filled him with joy, especially so when he saw his mother, Sara, running to greet him. She threw her arms around him and kissed him several times. In the process, Joshua dropped his crutch, but so strong was Sara's hug that he didn't need it.

"I am so happy to see you, my son! I missed you and thought of you every day. Let me look at you. Hmm, you look terrible, but nothing that a bath and my cooking could not cure." She picked up his crutch and together they made for the house. "Did you see this Jesus? What was he like?

Did you speak to him? Judging by the look of you, you have not eaten much since you left here. We will fix that."

Sara kept up a steady stream of questions, including news of the farm, the birth of a child, sales by Nathan, Avram's health, and on and on…

As he expected, Joshua barely got a word in beyond, "Yes, no, oh." She was ecstatic; Joshua was overwhelmed, but it felt good to be home. That evening Joshua and Avram were treated to a special feast with roast lamb, toasted wheat cakes, and of course, honey, in addition to the daily fare of olives, dried fruits, grapes and figs. Over many cups of wine, Joshua relayed his journey: the kindness of strangers, and the hostility of others, his climb up the hill, the injury when he fell, and his encounter with Jesus, followed by a chance meeting with a kind young woman, Avigail. At the mention of Avigail and the expression on Joshua's face, Sara could not help herself, "Do I detect that this meeting with Avigail is more than a chance encounter with a stranger?"

Shaking his head side to side and waving his hands in the same direction, "Oh, no, no, mother, she was so kind to me even in the face of fear by others; she gave me food and drink. There is nothing more," Joshua replied, slightly embarrassed.

But the blush on his face suggested something more, at least to Sara. She looked at Joshua sideways, and with a decidedly dubious expression, slowly uttered, "Hmm, yes, of course, Joshua, I see."

Avram also saw Joshua's awkward reaction. He said nothing, but raised an eyebrow.

Avram spoke about the farm. Looking directly at Joshua, he said, "Planting has been going well. I am very pleased, Joshua. You have done well for us. And as Sara reminds me daily that farming is a young man's occupation." Sara looked over at her husband with surprise. She thought that was as close as he had ever come to admitting that he was no longer the young, dynamic entrepreneur farmer. A brief smile, more of a smirk, crossed her lips.

As it was still early in the evening, Avram suggested that the three of them pay a visit to the workers. Their first stop was to see Nathan, the head gardener. Nathan hastily called the other farmers for an impromptu reunion celebration. Joshua was greeted with hugs, kisses and more wine. Indeed, it was a wonderful celebration. Joshua felt elated; he was surrounded by his parents and his extended family. He was home. The celebration lasted well into the late hours, long after Avram and Sara left. As happened previously, Joshua returned in the early morning hours, inebriated and barely able to stand up despite the crutch. Joshua managed to reach the house, and fell face forward on his bed with the crutch still under his arm.

It was the late morning before he stirred. When he awoke, he found himself covered with a blanket, his crutch propped against the wall and a cup of water beside the cot. Clearly the work of Sara. He arranged himself, and then went into the main room where Sara and Avram were seated as if waiting for him. Sara had a sympathetic expression; Avram shook his head, feigning disapproval, but said nothing. Not a word was spoken for several minutes. The silence was broken when in response to Sara's offer of food, Joshua sheepishly said, "No, thank you, mother. Perhaps, I will wait. I should see to the men."

With the help of Sara, Joshua got to his feet, albeit unsteadily. The sun was already high and the heat was rising by the moment, but the fresh air livened his spirits and helped to clear his head. He made his way to a stand of trees where he saw Nathan and several of the men obviously in a heated discussion. Upon seeing Joshua, the men stopped to greet him. He returned the greeting, "Shalom. Is there anything I can do to help?

Nathan replied, "Several of the trees are infected with worms. In the past, we simply picked the worms off the leaves, but this time, there are too many. Daniel recommends that we take the infected trees down. I cannot agree. There must be a better way."

Joshua looked at the trees; he picked several of the worms off the leaves, inspecting them closely. He thought for a long while. "Yes, I think I can help."

Joshua was now in command. "Here is what must be done. Daniel, go with several of the men to collect as much manure as you can. Jaziel, collect as much leftover cloth as possible. Nathan, here is a list of ingredients that I will require."

The three men were puzzled by Joshua's request but they respected the young man's knowledge and skills. They set off on their respective missions.

Several hours later, the farmers returned loaded down with Joshua's request. "Here is what we must do: build a mound of manure around each of the affected trees. Jaziel, cut the cloth in tenth of a cubit strips, soak each in vinegar, and then wrap them just above the manure mounds. Nathan had acquired the list of ingredients and a large wooden tub. Nathan, place a liter of warm water in the tub with soap, and then add some pepper, garlic and vinegar. Stir the mixture, and be ready to splash the concoction on the trees."

After several hours, the men completed their assigned tasks. Joshua said, "Watch as I apply the treatment. Be sure not to get the mixture in your eyes." With that, the men set about to administer the treatment. It proved to be long and arduous work but by nightfall, they had completed the job. They congratulated each other; it was a new experience for the men. The combined stench from the manure, vinegar, and the tub of the vile solution lingered on the farm for days. The men, including Joshua, were covered in manure and the vile mixture. Their wives were not well pleased, either with the odor, which now entered the homes together with the men, and the washing. Daniel's wife burned his clothes. Joshua also received something less than a warm welcome when he entered the house.

Sara was the first to react. "Goodness, Joshua, you stink! Whatever were you doing? Go into our garden, remove your clothes, and wash up. Avram could hardly stifle a laugh that brought a stern gaze from Sara. With a change of wind direction, the stench now permeated the house, much to Sara's chagrin.

The next morning Sara awakened Joshua. Nathan was waiting for him at the door. "Come my friend. See what you have done. It worked! The worms are gone." Joshua's curious but effective bug treatment had saved the grove of lemon trees. With the lingering odor still in the air, the women of the village saw for themselves what the men had accomplished. However, the women were not so impressed that it prompted them to ask why this accomplishment came with such a stench. Sara put her arms around Joshua, "I'm so proud of you." She then added, "Despite the smell." Avram nodded and patted Joshua's shoulder.

For the following year, Joshua and the farmers settled into a routine: planting, pruning, harvesting and selling.

Despite the hard work generally in the grueling sun, Joshua insisted that they devote time to their wives and children. They celebrated the Jewish holidays together, with Joshua leading the ceremonies. The farm had become more than just acres of fields and trees; it was now a close community of people who shared the same goal: selfless caring for one another in good and bad times, ensuring that the children were raised to be contributing members of this community and studying the Torah. It was indeed a time of peace and plenty.

CHAPTER 11

That peaceful life was suddenly interrupted in the early hours one morning. Joshua was roused out of a sound sleep when he heard a loud voice. As he gathered his senses, he realized that it was Sara who was calling out, "Avram, Avram, husband, wake up, wake up!"

Joshua rushed into their bedroom to find Sara cradling her husband in a flood of tears and kept calling Avram's name. Hearing Joshua enter the room, she turned, "See, Joshua, see! My Avram, my dear, dear Avram, my partner, my star." Joshua rushed to her side. Joshua could see that Avram was gone. He didn't know how long he had sat beside Sara with his arm around her. She cried until exhausted and fell into a fitful sleep. Joshua just sat there.

He remembered many years ago when he did the same thing for his other mother.

He waited for Sara to awaken. She was always there to help him to his feet. Now it was his turn. He helped her to the common room. "My dear mother, stay here and rest. I will notify the farmers." He took a long look at the man who had become his second father. He was a loving and caring man, much like his other father, perhaps not as demonstrative, but a good and loving man. Joshua bowed his head and whispered, "Rest in everlasting peace in the arms of our Lord God, my dear father."

Unlike his previous experience years earlier, the community of farmers was shocked and saddened by Avram's sudden death. Sara's grief was felt by everyone. Avram was more than a successful farmer; he was also a wise and generous owner-leader. With the Hebrew rituals completed, Avram was laid to rest in a grave alongside the flower bed. Unlike his previous experience with the death of his first parents, many of the farmers stood up to eulogize Avram. As a sign of their respect for him, they loved and respected Sara, who was constantly surrounded by the women well beyond the seven-day period for sitting Shiva.

Although Avram's death was an interruption of the daily rhythm, there was a farm to operate despite their loss. Planting, pruning, and harvesting would have to continue. It was now up to Sara to be their new leader. Late one evening, she and Joshua sat beneath a brilliant sky splashed with diamond-like stars. The cool air of the night enveloped them. After a long silence, Sara was the first to speak.

"Joshua, I know that I am to lead the farm; and in memory of our beloved Avram, I will do so. However, I cannot do it alone; you have been the real leader in the field. The women and I will see to the accounts. Please say that you will stay."

"Of course, Mother, I will stay. I will do whatever you ask of me."

"My son, you have been a blessing to your father and me. My life from this day forward will be a daily struggle; you will be a great comfort to me."

"Do not worry, mother. We have each other and a loving and merciful God to help and comfort us."

Sara put her head on Joshua's shoulder. "Thank you, son, thank you. Yes, we should give thanks to Him. You have become wise beyond your years."

CHAPTER 12

After a long and unsettled period, life on the farm slowly returned to normal. Joshua was now in clear command of the business. Every day Sara could be seen seated alone in the garden. Her lips would move, but there was no sound. To the farmers, it seemed strange; perhaps she had become overwhelmed with grief. But Joshua knew; she was praying. Notwithstanding her loss, each day, she still would bring fruits, bread, and honey for Joshua, who would sit with her and tell her of the day's events. After he returned to the fields, she would continue with her silent prayers.

Joshua witnessed the profound changes in the farm: the births and passing among the farmers; the younger boys took over from their fathers, who were getting too old to farm. Another great loss was the death of Nathan, the head gardener, shortly after Avram's demise. His wife, Deborah, and Sara had become friends in their mutual grief. Perhaps, the most visible change was the size of the farm. It was the largest in the area and the most productive. Traversing the five square kilometers now required another group of farmers to live on the other side of the farm to tend their end of the farm. So large were these two locations that they were now two "communities." Jewish holidays were no longer a small intimate occasion. Now, the two communities formed a large congregation that celebrated those holidays together. With the absence of a rabbi, Joshua had now become the de facto religious leader for these communities. Apart from his new role as teacher and leader, his most gratifying role was speaking to the children of the communities and sharing his garden with them. He slowly came to realize that he enjoyed his role as a spiritual leader to the communities more than as a farmer.

One afternoon as he sat in his garden, he remembered that it had been one year since he had encountered the man called Jesus of Nazareth. He often wondered what the prophet meant when he said, "We will meet again." That thought opened the door to a persistent feeling that there was something missing, that there was more to come in his life.

It came as a shock, the same crushing sorrow that he had felt upon the death of his mother years ago. After the end of a day of searing heat, Joshua retreated to the cool shade of his garden to meet his mother, Sara. As he approached, he saw her sitting there very still; her head was bowed, her chin resting on her chest. His first thought was that she was deep in prayer, but then it became clear when he saw that the rich brown color had drained from her lovely face. There was just a ghostly pale. His heart dropped; he closed his eyes and took a deep breath. Sara, his loving mother, was gone. He sat beside her, holding her cooling hand, and cried. She had not forgotten; on her lap was a bowl of bread, honey and fruit for him. To the very end, her love for her son was first and foremost in her life.

CHAPTER 13

Joshua was once again given the task of praying for and then burying his two surrogate parents. Upon their deaths, a cloud of sadness and grief hung over the farming community for the longest time. As Avram and Sara had no children, Joshua quickly realized that absent an heir, the regional governor of Rome would quickly claim the farm for himself. Roman rule was cruel and heartless. All the years of toil and sacrifice by Avram, Sara and all the farmers would come to a harsh end. His parent's home, now his, would be taken; all the hard-earned revenue would be confiscated; the farmers would be reduced to slaves driven to hunger and despair.

It came as no surprise to Joshua when the deputy to the regional governor came to the farm accompanied by a centurion and 20 armed soldiers. It was a show of force that could only mean one thing: the confiscation was imminent. These were hardened soldiers; any thought of resistance would be futile. This squad stopped in front of the house and formed a menacing line arrayed in front of Joshua and several of the farmers who had gathered alongside him. Before he could even greet them, the deputy and the centurion stepped forward.

"I am Gaius Fortis, deputy to His Excellency, Governor Lucius Andronicus, representative of our esteemed Imperial Emperor, Tiberius Caesar. At my side is Centurion Publius Antonius. This is to advise you that His Excellency wishes to know who the owner of this property is now after the death of the two Jews, Avram and Sara. According to the Law of Rome, the new owner must produce evidence of ownership. Without such evidence, the Law permits Rome to seize this farm and all its assets, including the farmers. I will return in a week for such proof of ownership." The Deputy turned away, and as quickly as they came, they marched off, leaving Joshua and the other farmers in stunned silence. The new farm leader, Daniel, asked, "Joshua, what do we do? Did Avram and Sara leave instructions?"

Joshua replied, "I don't know, Daniel. It was not a subject we ever discussed. I thought there would be more time for them to grow old and then make their wishes known. But this…" his voice trailed off.

Late one evening, several days after the encounter with the Roman delegation, Deborah, Nathan's widow and a close friend of Sara knocked on Joshua's door. She found him sitting alone in a room lit with only one candle; he was praying. He was so deep in his prayers that he did not hear her. Not wanting to disturb him, she waited just inside the open door. Sensing the presence of someone near him, Joshua turned and saw Deborah standing in the doorway. In that instant, it was unclear which one was more surprised. Joshua bolted upright; Deborah gasped and took a step back.

"Deborah, is there something the matter? Are you ill, frightened? What is it that brings you here at such a late hour?"

"I am so sorry, Joshua, I did not mean to disturb you. Before your mother died, she entrusted me with a document that was to be given to you after her death."

"Why have you waited so long to give it to me?" Joshua immediately regretted what he said; he felt guilt at sounding so harsh. "It is no matter, Deborah, I apologize."

She stepped forward and gave him what appeared to be a bundle of beautiful handwoven silk. Joshua gently took the package and unwrapped it, revealing a parchment scroll of the highest quality. He offered the silk wrapping to Deborah, and as he did so, he asked, "Do you know the contents of this document?"

"Yes, Joshua, I do. Your mother shared it with me, and asked me to make another copy in the event that this one was lost. Avram and Sara considered you in every respect to be their son; they loved you dearly." With that, Deborah stepped back toward the door. "I will leave you to read it."

"Thank you. I am grateful to you for holding this for me. May the God of Jacob bring you blessings."

Joshua sat on his cot and, for a few moments, let the scroll sit on his lap, hesitating to open it. He opened the scroll slowly and as he did so, he read it in a whisper:

LET IT BE KNOWN

IT IS OUR DECISION TO GIVE OUR SON, JOSHUA,
ALL THAT WE POSSESS WHICH INCLUDES
ALL THE LAND, THE LIVESTOCK,
THE CROPS, THE TREES
AND THE FRUITS THEREOF,
OUR HOME AND ALL ITS CONTENTS,
THE FARM AND THE REVENUES
ALL OF THIS, SO LONG AS HE SHALL LIVE.
IT SHALL BE HIS TO DISPOSE
AS HE ALONE DECIDES.

SARA BAT ISRAEL   AVRAM BEN MOSHE

He had to read the document several times before he could come to terms with ITS contents. He was now the rightful landowner. On the seventh day, the Roman soldiers marched on to the farm. Once again, Joshua had to endure the pompous deputy and his ritual introduction:

"I am Gaius Fortis, deputy to His Excellency, Governor Lucius Andronicus, representative of our esteemed Imperial Emperor, Tiberius Caesar. At my side is Centurion Publius Antonius. We have come to take possession of this farm and the laborers in compliance with the Law of Rome."

With the will in his hand, Joshua stepped forward, much to the surprise of the deputy. However, the centurion was not; he stepped forward toward Joshua. For the first time, Joshua noticed the man. He was hard-bitten and scarred, the result of too many battles. With his hand on his sword, he spoke, nay growled, "Do not take one more step further. I will take what is in your hand." Joshua gave the document over to the soldier, who passed it to the deputy.

As the deputy read the document, Joshua said, "Sir, that document is written proof that with this will, my parents have given me perpetual ownership of this property and everything in it. As you say, Roman law prevails in the Land of Israel, but as you also know, Roman law provides that a written will permits the transfer of property in the Land of Israel. Here is the will signed by my parents."

Frowning, the deputy read and re-read the document several times. He realized that he had been outmaneuvered and was not happy about it. His reply was brusque, which signaled to Joshua that this was not the end of the matter, "I will take this to Pontius Pilate, our esteemed governor in Jerusalem, to see if it conforms to the Law of Rome." He quickly turned and walked away, leaving the centurion and his heavily armed squad at a loss. The Romans had come prepared to use force to secure the farm, but there would be no battle today, and therefore, no plunder and no slaves. The centurion was furious; giving Joshua one last glare, he nodded his head slowly, his eyes narrowed and lips in a snarl. "This is not over. We shall meet again."

CHAPTER 14

The farm had now become a major business, and a significant tax contributor to the coffers of Rome. That ensured no interference from Pontius Pilate, at least for the time being. Now, without the fear of the Roman tax collector, Joshua hired as many laborers as the farm could support. He had become beloved by his workers. To them, Joshua was more than the master of the farm, but a kind, generous and compassionate man. Many approached him for advances or loans, to which he readily agreed. He took no servants, put on no airs and graces, dressed simply, and shared whatever revenue was left over from the sale of crops and livestock with the workers. He had also set aside plots of land for his workers to build larger homes of their own. He also established a school for the children to learn the Torah and farming. In a short time, his farm became a little village. It was a happy place where mothers and fathers watched as their children played and sang songs. On the Shabbat (a day of rest), Joshua led the families in prayer and readings of the Scriptures. When the children were in school, mothers assisted in planting seedlings and tending Joshua's garden, which had become a rather spacious site for solitude, tranquility and reflection.

So great was his love for the workers that he was often a guest in their new homes, and when he was home alone, the wives took turns in bringing a plate for him. He never refused. In fact, he found that he was gaining weight!

Joshua was in discussion with several of the farmers regarding next season's planting when one of the older boys approached Joshua, "Rabbi, there is a woman at the gate who says she knows you, and wishes to speak with you. She has a child with her."

Joshua was puzzled. A woman with a child? Asking for me? "Did you ask her name?" he replied.

"Yes, Rabbi, her name is Avigail."

Joshua's face lit up. "Ah, yes. Please show her to my home. Ask your mother to meet her and give her every courtesy. I shall be along in a few moments. Thank you."

After his meeting was concluded, Joshua hurried to his home to greet his guest. As he entered the house, Avigail rushed over to him, and dropped to her knees to kiss the hem of his robe. "Rabbi, I am honored that you agreed to see me."

He could not help but notice that her clothes were dirty and dusty; her hair was unruly and covered in dust, and her face looked pained and sad. As Joshua reached down and helped her to her feet, "I am just Joshua. I am not worthy of such an honor. I am so pleased to see you, but I must ask why you are here. And who is this beautiful child?"

"Joshua, your reputation as a caring master has spread throughout the land. I have come here to find work to feed my daughter. My husband died suddenly, and I have no means of support. This is my daughter, Sara." Although very thin from undernourishment, she was beautiful. Her dark eyes sparkled and her tiny face glowed. She was alert of her surroundings and kept staring at Joshua and his crutch.

The young girl's name struck him with both sadness and joy. In that instant, he found himself reminiscing about his mother, Sara. He leaned over and extended his hand; the fearless little girl eagerly grasped it. Without hesitation or embarrassment, pointing to his crutch, she asked him, "Why do you have this stick?"

Avigail reached for her daughter and said, "Sara, you should not ask such a question."

Pointing to his leg, he was impressed at the child's candor, "It is a crutch, child. It helps me to stand up as this leg does not work."

"Oh." Turning to her mother, she said, "Mother, I am hungry," was her simple response, characteristic of a child's innocence.

He looked over to Rebecca, the mother to one of the farm boys. She had been attentively listening to this exchange. Joshua remembered the young woman's generosity and compassion. "Rebecca would you kindly find food for the child. I need a few moments to speak with her mother."

Rebecca reached out for Sara who upon hearing the word "food" eagerly took the woman's hand.

With tears in her eyes, Avaigail reached out for Joshua's hand and said, "Thank you, Joshua, thank you."

"I remember your kindness to me when I was thirsty and hungry," Joshua replied. He gestured for Avaigail to sit. Painfully, he lowered himself into a chair opposite the woman. "Tell me all that has happened since I saw you."

With a halting voice and through tears, Avigail told him of her husband's sudden death, her neighbors shunning her and their unwillingness to share their meager food supply. She had set out, not knowing where she would go and how to find food for Sara. She was forced to beg along the way. One passer-by suggested that she could find work at a large farm a little more than a day's walk. The owner of the farm, Joshua, was known to be a kind and generous master. Perhaps, she could find work there. It was then that she decided to journey here, hopeful that she could find work.

Rebecca returned with the child, Sara. "Mother, see what I ate. I brought some for you." She ran to her mother and handed her a plate of fruit and bread. In a gesture of gratitude, Avigail put a hand to her chest, "Thank you, Rebecca, I am in your debt."

Rebecca turned to Joshua, "Rabbi, both of these poor souls need to eat more, wash off the dust, and rest after their harsh journey. I would be happy to take them to my house."

"Thank you, Rebecca," he replied. He turned to Avigail, "Go with Rebecca, and refresh yourself. We will speak again when you are feeling better. In the meantime, know that you are welcome here."

Soon thereafter, with the help of the women and the generosity of Joshua, Avigail and her daughter, Sara, were settled into one of the smaller cottages on the farm. She was a conscientious, hard worker who often joined the men to tend the crops whilst Sara attended school.

On a pleasant morning, as Joshua sat in his garden, he saw Avigail approaching him. "Good morning, Rabbi. May I speak to you? I need your wise counsel."

"Of course, Avigail. Is everything all right? You look sad. Is Sara well?"

Slowly and hesitatingly, Avigail began to speak, "I have been asked by Noah to be his wife. I am confused. Sara needs a father. What should I do? Rabbi, may I have your permission?"

Joshua replied, "Yes, I know Noah. He is a good man and would make a good husband and father. Marriage is a life-long, loving partnership. If you are ready to enter again into such a relationship, then you do not need my permission. You have my blessing."

Several days later, Noah asked permission to see Joshua. "Rabbi, it is my intention to marry Avigail. May I have your permission?" At the same time, he presented Joshua with a *mohar* (a dowry), the traditional gift to a girl's father to confirm the marriage, saying, "Rabbi, Avigail sees you as her father. Please accept this *mohar*."

Joshua smiled at the thought of being considered a father as he accepted the *mohar*. "Yes, Noah, you have my permission and my blessings."

Several weeks later, the wedding took place in the common area. Joshua presided over the brief ceremony, after which there was a celebration with songs, dancing, food and wine.

In a short time, Avigail, Noah and Sara settled into their new life, and became true members of the farm family. Avigail was a devoted wife; she bore another child, a son, whom they named Joshua to honor his namesake. The child Joshua was delighted to know that he had an 'uncle' with the same name, and took every opportunity to say "Shalom, Uncle Joshua." Despite suggestions from his parents to use the term of respect, "Rabbi," the young Joshua never stopped referring to the other Joshua as "uncle." And the elder Joshua never corrected him either.

It was a glorious spring day in the valley; the air was clear and crisp; birds were singing in the trees. It was spring on the farm; the planting had been completed. It was time to celebrate and pray for a good harvest. The families gathered in the common area and began their celebration by offering prayers and biblical readings led by Joshua, who was now recognized not only as the farm's master, but also its religious leader, the rabbi. He began the ceremony:

"Our Lord God has given us an abundance of blessings, an abundance of grain and fruits, and abundance of peace and love, an abundance of health and an abundance of children for the future. Truly, our Lord has chosen Israel as His garden. Let us raise our voices in gratitude."

He then read passages from the Bible,

"Sing we merrily unto
God, our strength; make
a cheerful noise unto the
God of Jacob."

"So your barns will be filled with plenty
And your vats will overflow with new wine."

"Then I shall give you rains in their
season, so that the land will yield its
produce and the trees of the field will bear
their fruit."

"Let us worship the Lord in song," The farmers and their families sang songs of joy and praise in tribute to God and thanksgiving for His gifts, the numerous blessings on the farm, the farmers, and the livestock and for a successful crop.

As Joshua listened to the singing, he was elated. He long ago abandoned the idea of a wife and family. As he looked at the men, women and children, happy and joyful, he concluded that his family consisted of the workers, their families, the farm animals and the many trees, shrubs, flowers and, and of course, the birds. At that moment, a thought occurred to him. Unbeknownst to anyone, this was also the day that Joshua recognized as his birthday; he reckoned that he was now 30 years old. He silently thanked God for Avram and Sara, for bringing him to the farm and for his good fortune.

CHAPTER 15

Two years passed. As he got older, he found that his withered limb pained him more often, but he bore it without complaint. The business continued to flourish. He was an astute businessman, and in the course of the years, had acquired more land for crops and livestock.

By any measure, he had succeeded in life. And yet, for all his good fortune, Joshua realized that there was something missing in his life.

As had been the case for weeks now, Joshua found himself awake in the middle of the night. It wasn't from bad dreams; no, just a gnawing feeling that there was something just out of his reach. He couldn't put words to it; they seemed to be draped in a cloud. All he had to do was to pierce that cloud; then all would be clear. He would know his destiny.

In the still of the night, Joshua strained to hear but there was absolute silence. The stillness had settled like a blanket on the farm. There were no whispers in the darkness: not a leaf stirred, not a night bird. He raised himself from his bed and hobbled outside. He was momentarily overwhelmed by the sight of the deep heavens. *How mighty is the Lord,* he thought. In that moment of awe, Joshua felt as if God had taken a handful of stars and cast them across the sky. For many long minutes, he looked up into the sky and marveled at the breathtaking beauty. Suddenly, it came to him: *is this a sign from God?* It was then that he remembered his encounter with the itinerant preacher, Jesus of Nazareth. *Could this possibly be the key to his search? Was this the simple answer to his restlessness after all: Jesus?*

From several of his workers, he continued to learn of the prophet's miracles, his sermons, and the growing number of followers. He had heard of this man's simple message of love, mercy and compassion for the downtrodden, the sick, the homeless, and those reviled as sinners.

For the next few days and weeks, he had become consumed by the thought that somehow, the answers for him lay with this holy man. He prayed for guidance and read the scrolls, all in the hope that the answer would tumble down like an avalanche. He was frustrated that the moment of enlightenment did not happen, but that only fortified his resolve.

One morning after a sleepless night, as he set out to supervise a tree pruning, one of the workers came to him to tell him of the news that Jesus was now on his way to Jerusalem to teach and to pray. It wasn't in a burst of heavenly light, or a chorus of angels or flaming chariots racing across the sky. It was more like a spark that had been growing for these years, and was now growing into a flame that revealed the mystery that had eluded him. He now saw what God's plan was behind that cloud. Joshua realized what was missing in his life. The answer was simple! His life and destiny were connected to Jesus. It was God's will.

He made his decision. He would leave the farm to find Jesus in Jerusalem. However, at the same time, he could not just abandon the farm. Surely the Romans would learn of his departure, and descend on the farm like vultures. Everything that Avram and Sara, and the other farmers who had devoted their lives to building the farm would be lost, but he was irrevocably committed to his decision. He prayed for guidance.

CHAPTER 16

For several days, Joshua did not leave his home. The workers became concerned that their master had fallen ill or worse. Several of the workers came to the door of his house, and called out to Joshua. There was no response. They were now convinced that something disastrous had befallen him, but they were at a loss. One member of the group asked no one in particular, "What should we do? It is not right that we enter the rabbi's house without his permission. Let us call one of the women. They will know what to do." They summoned Rebecca who came with Avigail and her daughter, Sara. Shaking her head, Rebecca spoke first, "Why has no one entered his house? He could be seriously ill." She beckoned to Avigail, "Come, Avigail, let us see what has occurred."

Both women, with little Sara in tow, entered Joshua's house. Despite it being almost mid-day, it was dark and cool. It was quiet, too quiet. Rebecca whispered to Avigail, "Something is not right. Let us go into his bed chamber." When they got to Joshua's room, they saw that it was almost dark; there were no windows. What light there was revealed Joshua kneeling at his bed, his crutch beside him. His face was buried in his hands, and several scrolls were lying on the bed. They heard him whispering, "Oh God of Abraham, I place my trust in thee. Lord, be my lamp in the darkness. Your infinite wisdom will show me the path I must follow."

Joshua heard their footsteps; he stopped his prayer and turned to his three visitors. Before, he could ask why they were there, little Sara came rushing to his bedside, and threw her arms around him, "Uncle Joshua, Uncle Joshua, can I tell you a secret?" The girl bent over, oblivious of the gravity of the moment, and whispered something in his ear. Joshua turned with tears in his eyes, but smiling, "Yes, my child, you are right. Let me see." With that, Joshua took hold of his crutch, stood up, and took Sara's hand.

As he and Sara walked past, Rebecca started to ask a question, "Rabbi?" Joshua looked over to the two women and whispered, "It's a secret." With that, Sara and Joshua walked out. Rebecca and Avigail were left standing in the dark room, bewildered. They decided not to follow, but as they walked out, they saw Joshua hobbling and holding Sara's hand while the little girl was looking up at him and chattering away.

Several more days passed as Joshua struggled with his decision. Perhaps it was a premonition or some unspoken communication between them, but from that point on, he was always accompanied by Sara. They walked the fields together and sat in his garden as he pointed out the blossoms, bugs and bees. The birds seemed to understand and were not afraid. Joshua handed her a little piece of bread and suggested that she put out her hand in front of her. No sooner did she do so that a little bird flew in and alighted first on Sara's shoulder and then on her hand. She squealed with delight and asked Joshua for more pieces of bread.

It was a beautiful sunny morning, a morning that would change his life forever. The fragrance of the wine and oil presses filled the air; birds were sitting in the trees aimlessly singing their unique songs; the flowers opened their petals as if in anticipation of Joshua's impending announcement. He called the workers and their families together. Gentle Sara was by his side. Except for the Jewish holidays, such a meeting in the middle of the day and workweek was most unusual. As he welcomed them with a "shalom," he seemed different in some way; the expression on his face was almost serene. A silence fell over the families as they waited for him to speak.

"My beloved friends, I have had the privilege of the love of parents who took me in when I was no more than a beggar on the roadside. Avram, my father, gave me purpose, first as a laborer and then as the master of this farm; Sara gave me the most precious gift of all: she became a loving mother, and in doing so, enriched my life beyond words. You have become my family, the brothers and sisters that I never had, and that too was a gift from Almighty God. And more recently, I have become an uncle to Sara, daughter of Noah and Avigail. She too has been a blessing.

After much reflection and prayer, our Lord God has helped me to realize that my life must take a different turn, and that turn will take me away from you. My decision to leave you weighs heavy on my heart, but despite the anguish in making this decision, I am convinced that the remainder of my life lies with Jesus of Nazareth."

The farmers were stunned. *How could this be? What will become of us? The Roman vultures will surely descend on us. Those of us whom they don't kill will become slaves.* The silence was broken by Noah, "Rabbi, what are we to do? You have been our master, friend and rabbi. If it is the will of God, we support your decision to become a disciple of Jesus, but I fear that when the Roman Governor learns of your departure, our lives and the farm will be at their mercy."

With that, Joshua reached down and took a scroll that Sara had been holding and held it up for all to see. "Do not be afraid, I have seen to that," he replied. "I have prepared this document that the procurator from Rome has now presented to the governor. It has been approved by Rome and has been recorded. No one will be able to take this land from you."

Slowly, he began to read the scroll.

LET IT BE KNOWN

*I, JOSHUA SON OF SARA BAT ISRAEL AND
AVRAM BER MOSHE*

*DO CONVEY ALL TITLE AND OWNERSHIP OF
THIS FARM AND*

ALL THAT I POSSESS, INCLUDING

ALL THE LAND, THE LIVESTOCK,

THE CROPS, THE TREES

AND THE FRUITS THEREOF,

MY HOMEAND ALL ITS CONTENTS,

*THE FARM AND ALLITS REVENUES TO THE
FAMILIES IN EQUAL PROPORTION SO*

*LONG AS THEY SHALL LIVE AND SHALL
SURVIVE TO THE SUCCEEDING GENERATIONS
WITHOUT LIMIT. THIS GRANT CAN BE
CHANGED ONLY BY THE UNANIMOUS VOTE
OF THE FAMILIES. A FAMILY WISHING TO
LEAVE THE FARM MUST SURRENDER THEIR
SHARE TO THE REMAINING FAMILIES.*

JOSHUA BEN ISRAEL

PREPARED BY: PROCURATOR SERVIUS SULPICIUS GALBA IN THE NAME OF HIS HIGHESTY MAJESTY AND LORD GOD. TIBERIUS CAESAR AUGUSTUS

CHAPTER 17

Although the farmers were now assured of their freedom and their future, they were still exceedingly sad. Joshua met with the farmers to give them final instructions regarding the business of farming. To the children, he reminded them to look to the Torah, to pray, to respect their parents and each other, and to play and enjoy their youth. To Sara, he entrusted his most prized possession: the garden.

That night despite the sadness, the farmers prepared a feast in his honor. It would be their last dinner together; they knew that they would never see him again. Although they tried to maintain brave faces, there were many tears shed and numerous pledges of prayers. One by one, each family said their good-byes. Joshua was now alone in the darkness. Those feelings of loneliness surfaced after so many years; tears welled in his eyes. He remembered Avram and Sara, mother and father to him; his first encounter with Sara on the road after the attack by the robbers; the days laboring in the hot sun pruning plants and later harvesting. And then there were the feasts for religious holidays and the harvest and the singing and dancing. For long moments, he was overcome with a profound sadness. So many more thoughts swirled around in his head, but there was no doubt. This was the right thing to do. He turned and went back to his room.

He looked about and saw the mementos that he had collected over the years. There were many gifts from his parents, mostly from Sara, his mother: several pairs of sandals, robes, a necklace with a pendant of gold inscribed with a Star of David, and a ring with a coral gemstone. Perhaps the most precious gift was the blanket woven by Sara shortly after his arrival on the farm. He realized that he would have to leave all these possessions behind, thus being able to free himself from the bonds of this material world in anticipation of his new life. He would use his freedom to take up the life of a poor mendicant, a monk, and follow the example of Jesus and his disciples.

It was late in the night before he could sleep. Thoughts like shooting stars burst across his mind and then disappeared. As he lay there staring up at the ceiling, doubts began to swell. *Am I doing the right thing? Could I not contribute to God's work by leading the farm as their master and rabbi? Am I ready to lead the life of a poor disciple? Could I not be a disciple of Jesus without abandoning my current life?* Slowly, feelings of anxiety and even fear began to creep into his thoughts. He was about to make the most important decision in his life, but he did not know what would be awaiting him. He really didn't know much about this man Jesus of Nazareth, either. True, he was a holy man, perhaps even a prophet. But secretly, a part of him hoped that this night would never end, thereby relieving him of the burden of such a fateful decision.

But the morning did come.

He heard the song of one lone bird chirp to break the silence. It seemed to Joshua that it was speaking to him, waiting for him to decide. His struggle with a decision was now put to the test. It was now or never. As he lifted

himself from his bed, he remembered a passage from the
Bible,

**"When I am afraid, I will trust in you. In God, whose
word I praise, in God I trust; I will not be afraid."**

In that moment, it became clear to him that God had
intervened. He had asked Joshua to take up the path to
follow Jesus. Grabbing his crutch, he raised himself from
his bed. He pulled Sara's blanket from the bed and
wrapped himself in it. He could feel her warmth and her
love. It was as if Sara were saying to him, "Go. This is your
destiny." He picked up a bag with some food. He then took
a last look around him and imprinted it in his mind. It was
a painting that he would always remember.

He then stepped out into a serene morning, that period
between night and day, the time when the sun began to
turn the sky from gray to a pale blue. The trees and the
fields were still draped in the blue-gray morning light. The
one lone bird continued its aimless melody. It was then that
he heard a familiar voice, "Uncle Joshua, Uncle Joshua."
Little Sara ran up to him and gave him a hug around his
leg. "Are you leaving, Uncle Joshua?" Before he could

answer, many of the farmers emerged from the dim light and surrounded him. One after the other, they came to him, "Shalom, rabbi, may God be with you." Joshua was speechless; he couldn't say anything more than "Shalom." It was time, time to go. The little girl sensed that there was more to this event than wishing Joshua a safe journey to the market. "Uncle Joshua, are you leaving forever?" Tears welled in his eyes as he looked into her searching eyes. Sara tugged on his robe, "You are coming back, Uncle Joshua, aren't you?"

With tears now streaming down his face, he gave her a kiss on her forehead and whispered to her, "I love you." He took a deep breath and turned away. He forced himself not to look back at the group of farmers, especially little Sara. He stepped onto the road, and within moments disappeared around the bend.

CHAPTER 18

He had been walking for three long and tortuous days. It had been a long time since Joshua had been challenged by such a journey. Despite the hard work of farming, he was unprepared for this journey. He had not walked such a distance in years. Each day, as the sun rose above the mountains, he could feel the merciless, searing heat on his face. He pulled his shawl to cover his head and face except for his eyes. His crutch, which had served him well for these years, had now become an instrument of torture. It chafed his underarm whenever he pressed his weight on it. He felt an excruciating pain with each step when his limp leg made contact with the ground. As a result, he was forced to stop repeatedly. The bruising under his arm had become unbearable; it was now an open sore, but he was determined to press on. He had only one thought: reach Jerusalem, whatever the cost.

However, on that third day, he could go no further. The constant pain under his arm and withered leg was too much; he could no longer tolerate it. He sat by the wayside despondent. He waited for another day before he would attempt to walk. He also realized that he had no more than one day of water, only a small piece of bread and several dates remaining. At first light of the fourth morning, he cried out as he tried to raise himself but the burst of pain under his arm stopped him. He looked at his arm and found that the entire area around his shoulder was red, and probably infected. He lowered himself beneath a tree and drank what little water he had left. The infection was now taking hold of him: he felt weak; he could barely lift his arms. He knew what a fever was and what it could do if left untreated. His fever was getting worse by the minute. The pain was unbearable, whether sitting or standing; the fever was now accompanied by a massive headache. Taken together with the heat, he felt himself slowly slipping into unconsciousness. The last thing he remembered was hearing the rustling leaves above his head.

He had no idea of how long he had been unconscious. As if in a dream, he felt drops of water on his lips. He stirred and then slowly opened his eyes to see a very old man leaning over him, holding a small cup. A parched throat and cracked lips made it difficult for him to speak. He opened his mouth and reached for the cup, trying to take more water from the cup. "Slowly, my son, slowly," the old man said gently.

The old man sat with Joshua for several hours, feeding him water and morsels of bread. Slowly, Joshua began to regain his senses and grimaced as he felt the pain in his head and limbs return. As the old man turned to his cart, Joshua pleaded hoarsely, "Please, sir, please don't leave me."

"Do not be afraid, my son, I am not going to leave you. I need some things if I am to help you."

The old man returned carrying several pieces of white cloth. Without a word, he washed Joshua's body; then placed one piece of cloth on Joshua's forehead. He took another piece, which he saturated with aromatic oil, and placed it around Joshua's shoulder wound. He then took more oil and gently rubbed into Joshua's face and lips. He made several trips to his cart to fetch more water, figs and bread that Joshua eagerly ate.

The old man finally said, "I will stay with you the night to change the bandages."

"May God bless you," was all that Joshua could utter.

"Thank you. May God be praised, return you to health," the old man replied.

Joshua was feeling decidedly better, but still very weak from the pain, sunstroke, thirst and hunger. Within a few moments, he fell into a deep sleep. The old man sat awake throughout the night, changing the bandages, and gently massaging Joshua's face and lips with oil.

It was nearly midday when Joshua woke up. Once again, he found the old man looking down at him. "*Subhan God!* You look so much better: your eyes are clear, there is no fever, and your wound is no longer as red." With a little help from the old man, Joshua managed to sit up. Yes, he did feel much better. "Sir, I don't know how to thank you. I don't have any money. I have nothing to repay you for your generosity. I am afraid that all I have to offer is my gratitude."

The old man smiled, "Your gratitude is a reward in itself for me."

"You have taken care of me; you saved me, and I don't even know the name of my savior."

"Qasim."

"My name is Joshua, sir," came the reply.

For the first time in several days, Joshua took careful note of his rescuer. Qasim's skin was dark and weathered like old leather. His tunic was white with a purple trim. He wore a somber-colored *keffiyeh*. His beard was white and long but well-combed. The most telling feature was his eyes, dark but gentle. His face seemed almost serene. Joshua thought to himself this is no ordinary wayfarer. The old man became aware that Joshua was staring at him. Qasim knew what the young man was thinking, "Yes, my son, I am a desert man and a member of a Bedouin tribe. I am traveling south to join my people in Egypt."

"Forgive me, sir, I did not mean to offend you."

"No offense taken my son, and please call me Qasim. The title 'sir' is only for dead men, and as you can see, I am very much alive."

"Sir, er, I mean Qasim, I have kept you from your journey, and for that I am truly sorry."

"For we Bedouins to help the helpless and to welcome all under heaven into our tents is a sacred obligation. God gives his blessing to those who perform an act of mercy. God willing, I will reach my home content that I was able to help a stranger. Thus, my friend, it is I who must thank you for the opportunity to do the will of God."

Joshua was struck for words. There was a long silence between both of them. It was Qasim who broke the silence, "Where do you live, my son? You came very close to death. You should take time to rest."

"Thank you, Qasim, I am on my way to Jerusalem to see the prophet they call Jesus."

"Ah, yes. I have heard of this man called Jesus. His reputation has spread throughout the land. It is said that he is the new prophet of Israel. You have risked a great deal for this chance meeting. May I ask why?"

"I did encounter him once before, Qasim, and I have thought about it every day since then. I keep hearing the words he spoke to me, 'We will meet again, Joshua.'"

"I see," said Qasim, "I must pass through Jerusalem on my way. You are in no condition to make the journey on foot. I will take you there."

Joshua was again at a loss for words. He wondered, *who is this man? Why is he so generous to strangers, especially one in my condition? Why did he just happen upon me and save my life? Was it a sign?* Before he could find answers to his questions, Qasim said softly, "My son, we are all travelers searching for answers. You are fortunate, indeed because at least you know the questions. Come, let us travel together. I too would like to meet this prophet."

"Thank you, Qasim, if it were not for your generosity, I am certain that I would not have survived this journey. I would be eternally grateful if I could make the journey with you."

Qasim helped Joshua into the bed of the cart as there was room for only one seat for Qasim to drive the two oxen. "I am sorry, my son, that you must ride in the rear along with my belongings," he said apologetically.

For the first time since his departure, Joshua had to laugh. "I never thought of myself as cargo, but better to be as one of these melons rather than the alternative, which is too awful to contemplate."

CHAPTER 19

It would be another two days before they reached the outskirts of the City of Jerusalem. They entered the city through the gate at the North Wall. Joshua had never seen such a large city. The walls surrounding the city were imposing, but it was the noise, the smells and the hordes of people that were overwhelming for him. Poverty and wealth melded together like a rough but colorful tapestry. It was only a moment before Joshua saw the large contingent of Roman soldiers; they were everywhere. They eyed the two travelers with suspicion and greed. Here was a cart loaded with food, cloth and other valuables led by a bearded old man and another much younger man seated in the rear among the goods. It would be easy to take everything from these two and dispose of them. Who would stop them? They were underpaid, living in a country they hated, and performing duties more like jailers than fighting soldiers. They did not need any pretext to stop them. Judging by the dress of the old man, it was clear that he was a desert man, a people that the Romans hated even more than the subjugated Jews. Qasim knew only too well that the Romans had committed indescribable horrors in their plan to conquer the known world. Qasim had warned him about the cruelty of the soldiers, but Joshua had his own experience with them when they stormed onto the farm after the death of Avram and Sara demanding that the ownership of the farm be turned over to the Roman governor.

Not wanting to draw too much attention, Qasim and Joshua kept to lesser-traveled streets, but it proved to be an unnecessary precaution. A Roman centurion stepped out of the shadows, flanked by six legionaries armed with swords and spears. The centurion, a tall burly man, ordered Qasim to stop.

"Who are you? Where are you going?" the gruff leader asked. Without waiting for an answer, he ordered them to get out of the cart. Qasim quickly climbed down; for Joshua, it was a different matter. As Joshua struggled to get out of the rear of the cart, the centurion, not satisfied that Joshua was moving fast enough, ordered one of his men to drag him out.

"When I speak, you will obey, Jew, or face the consequences!" roared the centurion.

"But sir, I am ...." Before Joshua could finish his sentence, one of the soldiers took hold of him, and violently threw him out of the cart. He landed on his shoulder that was still bandaged, and hit his head. For a moment, Joshua lost consciousness. Blood was flowing from a gash on his forehead.

"Get up!" the centurion bellowed. He grabbed Joshua by his hair and tried to lift him, but to no avail. Joshua just kept collapsing. Thinking that the young man was being obstinate, the centurion ordered one of the legionaries to punish him. He called out to one of the legionaries, "The flagellum!" The soldier took out a lead-tipped whip from his belt, and repeatedly whipped Joshua. The whip tore into Joshua's back, causing more pain and bleeding. Joshua cried out, "Please, sir, please, I am...."

"This will teach you to obey, Jew," shouted the officer, not only as a punishment to this man but also as a warning to the crowd that had gathered and watched in silence.

Qasim rushed over to the centurion, "Primus Pilus, please, I beg you. He is lame; he cannot stand without assistance."

The centurion, satisfied that sufficient punishment had been administered, ordered the legionary to stop. The centurion turned to Qasim, "Take him." Qasim lifted Joshua into the cart; he was bleeding profusely and now semi-conscious. As Qasim was about to climb back on the cart, the centurion grabbed him and spun him around. His face was inches away from Qasim's, so close that he could smell the soldier's revolting breath. He hissed, "For my trouble, you will give me all that is in your cart. Be grateful that I don't take that as well." He signaled to the six legionaries, who promptly pushed Joshua's limp body aside and unloaded everything. Qasim said nothing. He slowly climbed back into the cart and drove off. When he was out of sight of the legionaries, he stopped and climbed off the cart to see to Joshua, who was now awake and moaning from the pain. Several of the bystanders who had witnessed the all too familiar brutality of the Roman military came over to Qasim to offer assistance. They carried Joshua into a small house where several of the women tended to his wounds. Although in a great deal of pain, Joshua struggled to speak these few words, "Please, I must see him."

The bystanders turned to look at Qasim for a possible meaning. "He has come to see the prophet," he responded. "Have you heard of this man they call Jesus?"

One of the women replied, "Oh, yes, we have heard. All of Jerusalem has heard. He is expected to arrive from Bethel in three days' time."

Joshua heard the exchange. "Thank God," he whispered. He then closed his eyes and, although still in a great deal of pain, fell fast asleep.

The following three days passed too slowly for Joshua. Although still in pain, he was recovering quickly. Qasim had sat beside Joshua's bed, his eyes closed and silent. But on the second day, the women found that Qasim was gone. Joshua repeatedly asked where his friend was, hoping that he had not fallen once again into the hands of the Romans. On the third day, to Joshua's surprise and relief, Qasim appeared at Joshua's bedside. He was smiling. That was a good sign.

"Qasim, are you all right? I was worried, and thought that you have been taken…"

"No, my son, I had gone to the east end of the city. There I found a large crowd that had gathered along the road waiting with great anticipation for the prophet Jesus. He is on his way from Bethel and will arrive through the East gate later today. If you can manage, we should leave now if you wish to see him before he enters the Temple."

"Yes, yes!" Joshua exclaimed. "Let us go now!" With that, he turned to the two women who had watched over him for the past days to express his gratitude, "*Toda raba.*" He then turned to Qasim, "Let us make haste." As he was leaving the house, he turned to the women, put his right hand over his heart and said, "Shalom."

CHAPTER 20

Qasim and Joshua made their way out of the city by the Southern gate. Fortunately, there were no legionaries to intercept them. To avoid being seen, Qasim took a path through the Kidron Valley that ran parallel to the wall of the city. As they approached the road leading to the East gate, they could see a large crowd. Qasim found a spot for the cart and then helped Joshua to the side of the road. Despite the pain, Joshua leaned on his crutch as he leaned forward to see this holy man. He could see Jesus in the distance riding on a donkey, followed by hundreds of his disciples. The people on the roadside were waving palm branches and cheering, "Hosha na, hosha na".

For Joshua, the prophet's progress was too slow. It seemed that Jesus stopped continuously touching someone or speaking to others. As he got closer to where Joshua was standing, the "hosha nas" became louder. Palm branches were waving like flags in a strong wind.

And then it happened...

There he was, right in front of him! This was the moment that he had waited for since his first encounter with the prophet. This was the moment. Jesus saw Joshua and beckoned for him to come to him. So great was his excitement that Joshua felt light-head at that moment. He nearly fell as he stepped forward. The crowd suddenly fell silent. It was as if time stood still for Joshua as he took several halting steps to Jesus.

Joshua looked up at the prophet into his dark but gentle eyes. He felt as if he were being pulled into another world. Jesus leaned over, and with a warm smile, gently took Joshua's hand. Joshua began to shake. Jesus said softly, "In five days, we will meet for the final time." Joshua felt as if the earth gave way under his feet. He fell to his knees. When he looked up, Jesus had moved on, and once again, Joshua heard the roar of the crowd. Qasim helped

Joshua to his feet. As they made their way to the cart, the people who witnessed the encounter between Jesus and Joshua stepped back to make a path for the two.

Qasim had decided that it would be safer to stay outside the city walls. They camped a short distance from the road. For most of the afternoon, Joshua had not spoken a word; and Qasim left him to his thoughts.

"Qasim, he said that we would meet again in five days for the final time. What do you think he meant by 'for the final time'?"

"I do not know, my son, perhaps it foretells of a momentous event in your life and his. We must be patient, but whatever it is, there are only four days remaining. You have waited so long for these moments."

CHAPTER 21

It was dark when Jesus left the Temple. Although his disciples were with him, the throng of people that greeted him upon his entry into Jerusalem had left the roadside. Joshua and Qasim had set up camp at the cart. First, the oxen were fed and given water, after which both men ate by the fire. Joshua had not said much since his encounter with the prophet. It was evident to Qasim that Joshua was thinking and, perhaps, praying; it seemed that he was on the verge of a momentous decision. Qasim left him to his meditations. It was much the same for the next four days.

They knew that it was too dangerous for both of them to re-enter Jerusalem. Most assuredly, the Romans would not let a second meeting go without more severe punishment or worse. Joshua could not walk the distance, and the cart would be recognized. It was decided that Qasim would go at night alone into the city to purchase food. On the third night, on one of his ventures into the city, he learned that Jesus's visit to Jerusalem was the talk of the city. Everyone had heard of the miracles that he performed: curing disease and other infirmities, including raising the dead. This notoriety, coupled with the large number of disciples who were singing his praises as the next Messiah, had come to the attention of both the Roman leadership and the Jewish Temple hierarchy, the Sanhedrin and the Pharisees. With all his preaching about the Commandments of God, love, peace, caring for the poor, the infirm, and the outcasts, it was clear to both the Romans and the Jewish hierarchy that he posed an imminent threat to the established order, particularly if the many poor and disadvantaged united. It might cause a rebellion led by this prophet claiming to be God's messenger on earth with swift and violent consequences. Action had to be taken.

While in Jerusalem, Qasim heard rumors that the holy prophet had to be stopped by any means. When he returned to the camp, he told Joshua all that he had heard. Qasim said, "Perhaps, this is what the holy man meant when he said that you and he would meet the "final time." Upon hearing Qasim's news, Joshua became agitated, "What can we do? We must warn Jesus that he is in danger. Tomorrow will be the fifth day that he said he would see me again."

Qasim replied, "I agree, but it is too late now. The Roman guards will be suspicious if they see us on the road at this hour. We should wait until morning. In the meantime, I will try to find out where the prophet will be tomorrow." With that, Qasim disappeared into the gloomy night. Inside the walls of the city, he slipped silently passed the guards who were fast asleep.

It was in the middle of the night when Qasim reappeared. Joshua was still asleep. "Joshua, Joshua, wake up. We must go now! The prophet was arrested earlier while praying in the Garden of Gat Shmanim."

Joshua replied, "Where were his disciples? Surely they could have overtaken a few legionaries."

"He was alone, my son. His disciples abandoned him for fear that they too would be arrested. It was one of his closest disciples, a man named Judas Iscariot who identified him to the Sanhedrin and the Romans."

Joshua frowned and shook his head. *How could they?* "Did you learn of his whereabouts now?"

Qasim helped Joshua to his feet. As they made their way to the Southeast gate, Qasim explained, "Yes, he was led to the palace of Joseph Caiaphas, the high priest, where he refused to speak. It is said that Caiaphas fears that Jesus might start a rebellion, causing suppression by the Romans. Caiaphas does not want an excuse for the Romans to intervene. I fear that Caiaphas will want Jesus eliminated."

It was still dark when both of them approached the palace of Caiaphas just as Jesus was being taken to the Sanhedrin, the high court in Jerusalem, for trial. Joseph Caiaphas, the president of this body, had already come to the decision that this man would have to die. He charged Jesus with blasphemy for responding, "I am," to his question, "Art thou the Christ?" Blasphemy was a crime punishable by death. The assembled members of the Sanhedrin agreed: Jesus was convicted.

Qasim and Joshua saw Jesus in the distance being led from the Sanhedrin to the palace of Pontius Pilate, the governor and supreme judge of Judea. As only the Romans could inflict the death penalty, Jesus was led to Pilate for yet another trial, this time under Roman law. By now, a small crowd had gathered in the street. With his hands bound and blindfolded, Jesus was marched to Pilate, where he was being pushed, insulted and beaten by his Roman captors.

"Qasim, is there nothing we can do? They cannot do this! He is a peaceful, gentle man. He does not deserve such treatment."

"My dear friend, I am afraid we are past the point of trying to assist him. Events have overtaken us," Qasim replied.

The trial before Pilate was conducted in public at the entrance to the palace. Qasim, Joshua and many citizens had managed to get close enough to hear the proceedings. After interrogating Jesus, Pilate told the members of the Sanhedrin, "I cannot find fault with this man, certainly not to warrant death."

Hearing Pilate's decision, Joshua was ecstatic, and was about to shout his support for the decision, until Qasim put his hand over Joshua's mouth. "Be silent! Shouting support will not change anything. It may make it worse for the poor man, and expose you as a supporter which would not go well for you."

Several of the members of the Sanhedrin, led by Caiaphas, and the Pharisees were not satisfied with Pilate's decision. They shouted, "He is a blasphemer! He must be crucified."

Joshua was astounded when Pilate ordered Jesus to be flogged with the flagellum. Unlike Joshua's experience with the whip, Jesus was whipped thirty-nine times, the official number of strikes that the Romans required – no more, no less. To exceed thirty-nine strikes would likely kill the victim. The maximum strikes left Jesus's back torn open, bleeding and exposing muscle and bone.

"Please, Qasim, can we not intervene? He has already suffered enough. This goes beyond cruelty. Can we say something, anything, on his behalf?"

Qasim shook his head, "Nothing."

Pilate ordered that Jesus be taken to Herod Antipas because Jesus was a Galilean, and therefore, under Herod's jurisdiction. With his hands tied, he was dragged, often stumbling and falling from the flogging. The guards lifted him to his feet, and with the flagellum, beat him all the more. Jesus was half-conscious from the loss of blood, the kicks and the whip. Joshua was horrified at the sight, but with Qasim's strong hand on his shoulder, he was restrained from doing anything.

Jesus was pushed, dragged and forced to stand in front of Herod Antipas. The meeting between Herod and Jesus lasted only a few moments. Herod asked Jesus to perform a miracle, but Jesus remained silent. After that brief encounter, he ordered that Jesus be returned to Pilate. Herod wanted no part of this affair for fear of repercussions from the Sanhedrin.

As no commoner was permitted in Herod's palace, Joshua was not aware of what transpired until he heard the Roman guards complaining about escorting a condemned man back to Pilate. One of the guards grumbled aloud, "Why do we not kill him now? He is surely going to die anyway."

Jesus appeared draped in a red royal robe evidently given to him by Herod in mockery of Jesus's claim that he was the Son of God. Qasim and Joshua stood in the shadows behind the crowd that watched in silent amazement. They could see Jesus being kicked and cursed for falling. At one point, the guards grabbed his arms and dragged him the remainder of the way to Pilate's palace. By the time they reached the palace, the sun had arisen, drawing a larger crowd. Qasim and Joshua were now able to go unnoticed in the crowd.

Pilate appeared at the doorway of the palace, where everyone could witness the proceedings. Caiaphas, together with the members of the Sanhedrin, had positioned themselves in front of the crowd at the base of the steps in full view of Pilate. Caiaphas and other members of the Sanhedrin shouted, "He is a blasphemer! Crucify him!"

Pilate realized that he was faced with a dilemma: release Jesus and earn the ire of the Sanhedrin, risking a rebellion, or have Jesus crucified, satisfy the Sanhedrin and keep the uneasy peace with them. He then turned to one of his centurions, "The sentence is death. You will take him to be crucified." Always the politician, Pilate, in full view of the crowd, put his hands in a bowl of water, symbolically washing his hands of the matter.

CHAPTER 22

It was late morning when Jesus reappeared, flanked by two centurions and a contingent of legionaries. Joshua gasped when he saw him. Still wrapped in Herod's royal robe, Jesus now had what could only be described as a crown, a crown of thorns. The Roman soldiers noted for their cruelty had fashioned a ring from a mulberry shrub known for its sharp thorns. The centurion placed it on Jesus's head.

While a crown of thorns caused him unimaginable pain, the crown of thorns was more about mockery than it was about pain. Here was the "King of the Jews" being beaten, spit upon, and insulted by low-level Roman soldiers. The crown of thorns was the final act of their cruel mockery by taking a symbol of royalty and majesty, a crown, and turning it into something painful and degrading.

Blood was trickling down his forehead and for a moment it seemed that Jesus was about to fall over. One of the legionaries kicked Jesus, "Move, king! We will escort you, king, to your death." With that, Jesus was taken to the West gate, where several soldiers were waiting with an enormous wooden beam. They untied his hands and placed the six-foot, 100-pound plank over Jesus's shoulders. This would serve as the cross member of the cross. It was so heavy that he buckled under the weight. The soldiers screamed at him to get up.

Jesus was being taken to Golgotha, a hill just outside the city gates, which was known as the "skull" – the place selected by the Romans for executions. Only about 600 meters to the top of the skull, it still was going to be a long and agonizing walk. By now, the road was lined with people. Jesus struggled to take his first step and fell again, one of many as he began the climb to the crest of the infamous hill.

Fearing that Jesus would die from the torture he had received, the centurion commanded that a bystander, Simon of Cyrene, assist the condemned man. No young man himself, Simon struggled as well. Joshua and Qasim, who were just outside the gate, saw the struggle. It was at that very instant that Joshua resolved to intercede regardless of the consequences. He looked at Qasim and was about to tell him about his decision, but Qasim already knew.

Qasim nodded astutely, "I know, Joshua. This is what he meant when he said, 'We will meet again.' This is your destiny, a destiny that is tied to his. You know what you must do. You also know that I cannot accompany you on this journey."

"Yes, Qasim, I am sad that it is here where we must part. You have been a loyal friend and protector. I can never thank you enough." He took a deep breath and said, "God bless you."

"May the Lord bless you and protect you, and be gracious to you; may the Lord shine his face to you; may the Lord turn his face to you, and give to you peace," he responded in perfect Hebrew.

Joshua taking Qasim's hand said, "Shalom." He took one final look at his friend, turned, and hobbled as fast as he could manage to the gruesome scene playing out in front of him.

CHAPTER 23

After a few painful steps, Jesus staggered and stumbled again and again. The screams and the whipping from the soldiers were no longer prodding Jesus to move any faster.

As Jesus reached the place where Joshua was standing, he faltered again under the weight of the heavy beam. Jesus fell, and this time lay prostrate unmoving in the dirt and filth of the road. Having been flogged, stoned and beaten with sticks, he could go no further. Without hesitating, and amidst the curses of the soldiers and the jeers of many of the bystanders, Joshua hobbled over to him. As he did so, a Roman legionnaire lashed a whip at Joshua. He winced with the pain. It ripped his shirt but he was undeterred.

Joshua ducked under the plank. He saw that Jesus was bleeding from his head where the Romans had placed the crown of thorns. His shirt was in tatters from the thirty-nine lashes he had received from the Roman legionnaires. It was clear to Joshua that Jesus would not be able to make it to the top of the hill.

Jesus was not moving. It appeared at first to Joshua that Jesus was already dead. As he lifted the beam, Jesus stirred. Joshua said to him, "I will help you, Lord. Let me take the weight." He then put his back under the massive weight of the piece of wood. As he strained to lift alongside Jesus, he saw that Jesus's face was stained with blood, tears and dirt, but it was more than the physical brutality that Joshua saw; there was a profound sadness and resignation written on his face. Despite the brutality and gruesome agonies that he had suffered, Jesus struggled first to his knees, and then with a determination borne of his divine mission, he got to his feet.

And then and only for an instant, time stood still. Jesus looked over to Joshua, and between the agonies he was suffering, he managed to push out these words, "Joshua, this day as you came to me, my Father will come to you."

And in that instant, Joshua felt as if he had been struck by lightning. He looked down and was overwhelmed to see that his withered leg was no longer the emaciated limb he had endured for his entire life. He had been cured, but there was little time to celebrate. He dropped the crutch, and for the duration of the struggle to Golgotha Hill, Joshua strained alongside Jesus to help carry the heavy load, and to pick him up when he faltered so many times. Joshua was amazed at this man's endurance. No ordinary man could endure such cruel punishment. As they walked, some supporters of Rome in the crowd spit on Jesus; others he saw were crying. The Roman soldiers jeered. "Now that there are two of you, hurry to your death, king. My belly is rumbling with hunger!"

CHAPTER 24

At mid-morning, after a long and tortured walk, they managed to stumble and crawl up the hill of the "skull." At the top of the hill, Jesus and Joshua were met by a group of Roman soldiers. They grabbed Joshua. The centurion sneered, "You are a fool, Jew. Go now. You are no longer needed." With kicks and a flurry of blows, one of the legionaries threw him to the ground. But Joshua stood up in defiance. It was then that the centurion looked more closely at him. The Roman leader squinted as if he were trying to make a connection. And then it came to him. "Aren't you the cripple we stopped together with that pagan?" The Roman looked at Joshua. He saw that the crutch was gone, and the man was standing on two functioning legs. He then said, "Yes, I remember. It *was you in the cart.*" Joshua said nothing; he continued to glare at the officer. The centurion couldn't put his finger on it, but there was something wrong with this picture. *A week ago, this cripple could not stand on his own, but now he stands upright.* He thought to himself, *how could this be? Is it possible that there was some divine intervention? If so, whose god?* He had never heard of his Roman gods performing such cures. Yet, he saw it. The man did discard his crutch while helping the condemned man who claimed to be the Son of God. However, he decided not to pursue this any further lest the brutes in his company of legionaries might start asking questions. He had to complete the task at hand: crucifixion.

Romans did not invent crucifixion. However, they have the dubious distinction of having perfected the various methods that were designed to inflict maximum torment completed by death. It was not just designed to kill the victim, but to produce a slow death with maximum pain and suffering. It was a statement by Rome that it would not tolerate dissent or opposition. Crucifixion also sent a message of shame to the family and friends of the victim. It was one of the most disgraceful and cruel methods of execution. Although crucifixion was not unknown to people, the crucifixion of this man seemed to deviate from the typical crucified criminals: slaves, revolutionaries, and those convicted of heinous crimes, but not a man preaching a message of peace, love and justice, and yet no one dared intervene in the case of Jesus. To do so would incur a severe punishment, including crucifixion.

Just off the crest of Golgotha stood a group of his disciples who could only watch in shock and revulsion. In the midst of this cluster stood two heartbroken women crying: Mary, Jesus's mother, and Mary Magdalene the most prominent disciple and often referred to as the "thirteenth apostle". Having witnessed his struggle up the hill, the women also knew that the worst was yet to come. Several women and one Joseph of Arimathea attempted to console Mary, Jesus's mother who kept repeating, "My son, my son."

The centurion approached them, sneering and demanding to know the whereabouts of Jesus's disciples, "So, are you the only ones loyal to this man? Where are the others they call his close followers? If they are so committed to his message, why aren't they here?" As he turned back to the crucifixion, he swung around and shouted, "They are cowards in hiding! So much for loyalty."

CHAPTER 25

Joshua watched in horror as the gruesome process of crucifixion began. The Roman soldiers threw Jesus to the ground and untied him from the plank. They then proceeded to pound 4-inch spikes in Jesus's hands. As he cried out with excruciating pain, the centurion pressed the legionnaires to complete their gruesome task.

The plank with Jesus's outstretched arms and pierced hands was then lifted onto the nine-foot wooden pole that was already in the ground. The guards then hoisted Jesus up the pole and tied it off with rope to form a crude cross. Jesus hung from this cross, bleeding and twisting in what must have been unbearable pain. Next, the brutish Romans took perverse delight in driving a large spike into Jesus's feet to ensure that he could lift himself to breathe.

Not satisfied with the physical brutality, they added a final insult to the itinerant preacher who spoke of love, peace and compassion. On the top of the pole, they fixed a sign with the inscription, "INRI" – *Isus Nazarnus, Rex Idaerum* (Jesus of Nazareth, King of the Jews).

Joshua had never witnessed such brutal and inhumane treatment. True, he had seen sacrifices of goats and cows as burnt offerings, but this barbarity was beyond Joshua's comprehension. He felt sick at the sight. The cries of agony and the pain etched on the Preacher's face were so horrible that Joshua could no longer stand by. What followed brought Joshua to this critical point in his life, and in so doing, sealed his fate forever.

'"Why do you do this? He is innocent! It is you who are the guilty ones," Joshua shouted.

The centurion of the soldiers approached Joshua slowly like a tiger about to pounce on its prey. He stopped within inches of Joshua's face. He looked menacingly at Joshua, and then shouted for all to hear, "He proclaims to be the Son of God. There is no god other than Caesar. Men have been crucified for less." He pointed to another man who was then screaming in agony as he was being hoisted on a cross alongside Jesus. With a coarse laugh, he said, "Do you see that man? He is going to be your god's companion."

The centurion turned and walked away to inspect this second crucifixion. Standing under the cross, the centurion called out to Joshua, "This man is a thief – just a thief – not a blasphemer like your friend here."

Joshua could not contain his anger any longer. "You and your god, this Caesar, are the blasphemers. Your ignorance and idolatry have condemned an innocent man." There was a foreboding silence as all the Roman legionaries turned first to Joshua and then to their captain.

The captain could see the other soldiers watching. He knew that if he failed to come to the defense of Rome after such a rebuke of Caesar, the captain himself could be crucified. The centurion was outraged, "Enough! Seize him!"

Immediately, two of the legionaries took hold of Joshua, and at the same time, kicked and punched him mercilessly. Was that enough to punish him? Did this ruthless thrashing satisfy the offensive outburst? The sergeant of the guard and the other soldiers looked at the captain, waiting…

The centurion knew what his men were thinking. He had to act. To release Joshua was a step too far, and would most certainly jeopardize him, particularly once Pilate heard about this incident. There would be no mercy even for a centurion. As a captain of the guard, he had earned a comfortable existence. If all went well, he would be able to leave this awful place and return to Rome, his family, and perhaps a promotion. He could not let this offense go unpunished.

Turning to Joshua, he sneered, "You helped him up this hill; you mock me; you defiled the name of our dear emperor. You shall have your wish. You will die alongside him." Turning to the sergeant, he pronounced the sentence, "This man has dishonored Caesar. The punishment is death. Crucify him!" The soldiers immediately grabbed hold of Joshua, beating and kicking him. After this thrashing, one of them took out the flagellum and proceeded to whip Joshua unmercifully amidst the shouts, "There is no god, but Caesar!"

It was now Joshua's turn to feel the torment, the agony and a painful death. As they did with Jesus, his hands were nailed to a heavy beam. The pain was unbearable; he cried out in agony as they hoisted him on a pole, after which they pounded nails into his feet. Even in the face of such pain, for a few seconds, he saw his life flash before his eyes. And then, in that instant, he realized that his whole life had been a journey to this place.

Joshua was crucified on the right side alongside Jesus. Throughout history, it is said that no one really knew the names of the two people who were crucified alongside Jesus. One, the thief, challenged Jesus to climb down from his cross if he were really the Son of God. The other, Joshua, looked over to Jesus and said, "Remember me when you go to meet your Father."

Jesus looked over to Joshua, and said through his final agonizing breaths, "Joshua, you will be with me this day in heaven." Jesus then raised his eyes to heaven and said, "Father, into thy hands, I commend my spirit." His head then lowered to his chest. Moments later, Jesus died.

At that very instant, day turned to night, lightning streaked across the sky, thunder roared and the earth began to shake violently. Houses collapsed, fires erupted, people fell as they ran, and the terrified Roman soldiers huddled in a hopeless attempt to save themselves.

In the midst of this chaos, someone was heard saying, "Truly, this man was the son of God."

Joshua could no longer breathe and could no longer feel any pain. He knew that his time had come. As he slowly slipped away, Joshua looked up and, with a faint smile, whispered, *"Yeah, though I walk through the valley of the shadow of death, I will fear no evil, for thou art with me; thy rod and thy staff, they comfort me."* He struggled for one last breath, and then his head rolled forward. Despite all that he had gone through his entire life, which ended with torture and crucifixion, the expression on his face was peaceful, even in death.

CHAPTER 26

Later that day, Jesus's mother, Mary, her sister, Mary Magdalene, and several of Jesus's followers came to take him down from the cross. They removed the ugly crown from his forehead and gently laid his battered body in his mother's lap for her to grieve the loss of her son. Mary's tears fell on Jesus's chest. Although she understood his mission in life, she was still his mother and it tore at her heart to see her son die in such a way. Mary Magdalene and the other followers who had witnessed the crucifixion could only watch and wait for Mary to come to terms with this terrible tragedy.

Jesus's body was carried to a secret location where it was prepared in accordance with Jewish law. He was then wrapped in a simple white linen. After the recitation of the *kaddish*, the simple prayer for the dead, the cave was sealed with a large stone.

It was dusk when they came back for Joshua's body. But it was not there. To this day, no one knows what happened to Joshua.

EPILOGUE

It was said that shortly after the death of Jesus and Joshua, one of his disciples, Joseph of Arimathea, witnessed an elderly man driving a rickety cart on the road north. He spoke to no one. In his cart, he carried a body wrapped in white linen. On the last leg of his long and tedious journey, the old man reached a farm near the village of Shiloh. As he approached, he could see a large house and numerous people working in the adjacent fields. Yes, this was the place that Joshua spoke of so often.

The residents of the farm had heard of the crucifixions of both the prophet Jesus and a disciple named Joshua. Qasim was met with a mix of sadness and relief. Their beloved Joshua had returned home from his quest. Qasim said, "Joshua was a gentle and compassionate man, a man on a lifelong search to find the meaning of his life that was fulfilled with his encounter with the prophet Jesus and ended with their crucifixion. Joshua went to his death, content in the knowledge that he had found his path to salvation. You should also know that he never stopped talking about his life here with all of you and his parents."

With a brief and simple ceremony, Joshua was laid to rest in his garden alongside his adoptive parents, Sara and Avram. It was a glorious day. The daisy flowers glowed in the sunlight; the sweet fragrances floated in the air. One young boy, Joshua, stepped forward. "He was my uncle Joshua." He hesitated for a moment stifling tears. "Shalom, shalom, Uncle Joshua. May the God of our fathers hold you in his arms."

But it was little Sara who had the last word, "I love you."

A FINAL WORD

My objective in writing this story was to put a name and face on an otherwise nameless person. I have named him Joshua. History has all but forgotten this Joshua, and the role he played in the Christian theology of faith. He was on a quest to discover the answer to an ageless question that confronts us all: what is the purpose of my life? The veil that shrouded the answer was lifted when he encountered the prophet, Jesus. His faith came to a climax as he joined Jesus in death on the cross alongside him. Sadly, the only biblical reference to him is "thief."

He never claimed to be a saint or a mystic, just a humble man whose simplicity and compassion brought joy to everyone he touched. He could serve as a role model for today's Christians owing to his unquestioning faith in Jesus Christ as the Holy Messiah.

Although a work of fiction, I have endeavored to insert Joshua into the context of real biblical events.

Finally, there is a small roadside stand on Route 60, the Ramalla Nabllus road, where the old city of Shiloh once stood. It bears the name, "Joshua's Fruit Farm.

About The Author

Philip Antony has drawn on his experiences from his multi-faceted career as a lawyer, business consultant and university professor. He has travelled the world where he was privileged to meet and interact with people of many cultures, which he has woven into all of his stories. He has produced a long line of young adult stories and adult novels in which his rich imagination and international experiences have created a cast of colourful, relatable characters and exciting adventures.

The underlying theme of his stories is the power of love, friendship and compassion that overcome the forces of hatred and division. Although his stories are works of fiction, his novels convey that contemporary message with excitement interspersed with warmth and humour. His work stands in stark contrast to the enmity and divisiveness we read about in our world today.